CW01084473

Stolen

Tales for

Cunning

Thieves

Part II

Written by Matthew Hillsdon

Self Published

First Edition

First published in Great Britain in 2023

Copyright © Matthew Hillsdon 2023

ISBN:978-1-7394963-0-2

A record of this book is available from the British
Library.

Cover illustration: Bobooks
Edited by: Emma Hillsdon

Five short stories from the world of Alidor

The World Builders
The First Apprentice
A Forgettable Feather
When The Shadows Returned
The Dragon and his Phoenix

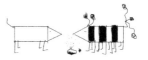

The
World
Builders

Stolen Tales

Long ago, before there were wars, disease and death. When the high elves were still young and the world mostly barren did the last true peace prosper. A peace the high elves would soon forget in favour of conquest and greed.

At this time Duniesa is no sprawling sparkling city, but a large town was all it had yet to become. Sweet and fair were most of the people here until the spring of their seventy third year. For these past years the high elves had worked alongside Norcea's World Builders. So now all about trees grew and green grass covered the lands around Duniesa. None worked closer with the Builders than Martha and Santra Dune. Of the first to fall to Alidor were they and had been to one another's side since they first stood tall and had even conceived a child. Not all were as content as they however, one called Inkark Urel had long despised the World Builders. He had won a following after leading a meagre force to defeat an invading army of dwarves who had tunnelled their way into high elf's lands. Saving Duniesa from its first major threat had lead many to heed his words, words that now went against Norcea's Builders.

'The north is green and our job here is done, to the south we should go. Their barren lands wait for us to claim as our own. Here is done and the first can have it, to the south the rest shall be free to explore. Free to shape as we see fit,' Inkark declared. In the centre of Duniesa he was speaking, with a crowd of hundreds before him who cheered hearing his words. 'What of the Builders and of Norcea's will, the north is ours brother. Given by the Lady to create a world for her own, why leave when the work is all but done,' Martha announced climbing up to join him on the stage he stood upon. 'Norcea's will is done, her first have their land, but what of the rest,' Inkark yelled as the crowd continued to cheer him and condemn her. 'For the beasts, that is why we don't cross the lake. Forget Norcea if you must, but they shall fight if you wish to take their lands. There is none of that strife here, nor war or sickness and you need not bring it brother,' Martha argued. Her words though were heard by only a few. Leaving the stage and the riled up and bustling crowd behind Martha ran to the ocean. There Santra worked with one of the World Builders on a small dock that had almost been completed. Foot long swaying necks and pale chalk like skin do the Builders have, making them easy to spot in a crowd. 'It's Inkark, he's rallying who he can to go against Elidom,' Martha declared running to the pair. 'He still wishes to pass the lake?' Santra asked.

'I believe he wishes worse than that,' Martha said. 'Come, we must find Avlor and speak with Elidom before this gets out of hand. Trycire, you and yours should get clear of here, head back to The Panisa,' Santra said. Referring to a hamlet most of the World Builders whose tasks were completed had begun retiring to. 'Leave, no. There's no need. The mastery of words will resolve this, as it has before. Wisdom is all they seek and by nightfall this will all have been resolved,' Trycire insisted. Wisdom though is the last thing Inkark and his followers sought and as the three of them made their way from the dock they were surrounded. 'Bind their hands,' one yelled while they were set upon. Bound and blinded they were dragged on their backs through Duniesa's streets.

Back to the stage they were taken where others in the same sorry state as they waited and Inkark marched back and forth before them. Suddenly Martha's blindfold was removed so she could see the beheaded bodies of the World Builders before her and Inkark's bloody sword. The pale heads bounced over the stage as Inkark paced up and down. While their beheaded bodies had been thrown to the baying crowd. 'What have you done?' She wailed as Trycire was pushed to his knees. 'No, Inkark, stop. This is madness,' Santra yelled as the sword fell. 'Do not fear brothers and sisters for just their blood will spill today. With it Norcea's control over us ends,' Inkark declared. Turning Santra saw beside him Elidom Godborn knelt, bloody and beaten he was. Another World Builder was then pushed from the crowd. His pale face showed an emotion the Dunes had yet to see upon a Builder. The sheer fear coating the being's face made Martha weep. 'Good, bring them all forth to face their reckoning,' Inkark yelled as a

young high elf lead the Builder onto the stage.
Inkark's sword was handed to him making Elidom
Godborn use what strength he had left to yell.
'Don't Jandor. Don't fall as he has,' but mere
words couldn't help. Forced on by Inkark and an
expecting crowd Jandor's arms rose and the
Builder fell before him. As the Builder's body
collapsed to the stage and its head rolled before
Santra, Inkark and Jandor were suddenly thrown
back by a great golden light that filled the centre of
Dunesia and within a portal opened. 'Avlor,'
Inkark roared as the light faded and he found the
stage was clear of all but he and Jandor.

'Return, we must return before he musters more to
his ludicrous cause,' Elidom said stumbling to his
feet. 'We can't Godborn, we hardly had the
strength to recover those here,' Avlor replied
gesturing to the Builders around them. 'Where is
Kuran, is he safe?' Martha asked.

'Safe as he always is in my care dear
Martha,' Avlor said as one of the Builders handed
her child to her. 'I was able to recover the La
Sore's young also, but they were not as lucky. Both

fought when Inkark's thugs came for them and died doing so.' With a deep sigh Avlor went on, 'Inkark has been planning this revolt for quite some time. His sympathisers attacked all loyal to the Builders. This here is all that's left.'

'If not return then what must we do,' Elidom said. 'Run,' Avlor replied. 'Run to the south, we will create a bridge over the Lavender Lake. With our skills and the Builders know how it would be a simple feat, but I fear Inkark has planned for this,' Avlor said.

'Let Inkark plan all he likes. Me and Elidom will take whoever's willing and hold his forces here,' Santra said.

'That's suicide, you saw the people. He has all of Dunisea to his back and the Builders can't fight, nor us. We don't know how to fight a war,' Martha said. 'They will already be marching for the gorge and will travel at double our speed, triple even. The Builders are hardly the speediest of beings,' Avlor said.

'You should leave us, go on and save yourselves,' Zolan said joining them. She was a World Builder and because of recent events was now the oldest of her kind. 'We have a pod in the south we were using to observe the beasts, we will flee there.'

'That's not happening,' Elidom declared. 'What does your foresight show you Avlor? Avlor.' Going to him Elidom realised Avlor's eyes had turned black. All of a sudden he grabbed Elidom's shoulders and yelled. 'Run, we can do nothing but run. They have one who watches us from up high. A god favours them,' Avlor said.

'What, why would Norcea wish her own Builders slaughtered?' Santra asked.

'It is not her that blesses their cause, but another. One who controls power we cannot face and survive.' As Avlor spoke the colour returned to his eyes but the darkness that rested within them now crept over the sky. Crackling black clouds blew overhead and within monsters summoned by shadow magic prepared to descend on what was left of the World Builders.

Elidom and his allies were banished. Every World Builder that could be found had been put to death, but still Inkark Urel raged. 'Wipe them away,' he bellowed to the others he had plotted the Builder's downfall with. 'Wipe away all trace, wipe away all memory of them. High elf's rule their lands now and our victory would be certain if not for your lying eyes.'

'It matters little, Elidom is gone. We can march south when we wish,' Jandor Grimis replied. 'He is far from gone, and with Avlor Tranem loose more strife will they cause. Already they rally others to aid them, they will not let us pass south without a fight like we had planned.' Tillamun Arch replied. 'Tillamun's correct, so is it you or your eyes that fail us Grimis?' Inkark said as he sauntered to Jandor's back. He and three others sat around the table that Inkark had been circling. Tillamun Arch was the master bookkeeper at the high elf's vault and a mage of great renown. Famsa Soper the only female of the group brought with her the following that now praised Inkark's revolt. While Samuel Pearce and Jandor Grimis had both been picked for their skills alone. Not all of their skills had been given to them by birth however, such as Jandor's gift of foresight that allowed him to see possible futures. Inkark however now felt this skill may be used better by another. Placing his hands to Jandor's shoulders he said. 'Your foresight was meant to be our greatest gift. With it we should have been able to deceive Avlor, but you failed us Jandor. Each here has been blessed by our all knowing Master. To Famsa goes the gift of knowing the minds of all she can see, telepathy if you will. Tillamun was granted a great tome to further his abilities and mastery of the shadows. Samuel was generously blessed with incredible strength so he might reach his true potential as a warrior. While I can recover from any wound. Our Master gave us these gifts to act as a vengeful fist and if one fails we all fail in his eyes.'

'I didn't fail, I told you my eyes only show me possible futures and I told you all I saw,' Jandor replied as Tillamun revealed a book clad in black cloth. 'You don't need that.'

'You must make amends for your failure Jandor,' Tillamun replied.

'What's he talking about?' Jandor snapped as he attempted to rise from his seat. Inkark's hands though held him down. 'If you cannot make good use of the eyes our Master gifted you, another will,' Inkark went on grinding his teeth as he spoke. Jandor began to struggle but Famsa helped hold him still as Samuel drew a dagger from his belt and forced Jandor's eyelids open. Inserting the dagger beneath his eyeball Samuel ignored Jandor's pleas as he popped the eye from its socket. The other quickly followed leaving Jandor blind and writhing on the floor in agony. Opening the black cloth book Tillamun spoke words that didn't belong to any of this world and as he did shadows spawned around the book. One floated over the table to the bloody eyes while another moved to Jandor. With the shadow's touch Jandor's cries ceased but only for a second. Even greater cries of anguish followed as the shadows ran over his skin to his face. Spreading over his cheeks to his eyes the shadows burrowed their way into his skin. Flowing like a prison door over his empty eye sockets until with one violent tug they fused together. Fading shadows left black wire in its place and Jandor huddled on the floor in excruciating pain. The other shadows had quickly engulfed the eyes on the table and as they touched them they went pure black. Carried to Tillamun's eyes they were and there they replaced his own. 'Did it work, can you see them?' Inkark asked.

'Yes I see, I see so much of this world and more. Wasted these eyes were on him,' Tillamun scoffed as more shadows poured from the book. 'Our Master sees us, he watches us and has blessed our path. Elidom has his followers fleeing with Avlor and what's left of Norcea's Builders. Foresight shows me they go to the only trees the south has. Seems you were right Inkark they mean to take it for their own.'

'What of Elidom, Avlor is nothing but a fool and easily dealt with along with Norcea's own,' Samuel said.

'He and the Dune's aim to block our path, but without the La Sore's might they will be little trouble,' Tillamun replied.

'Send the Master's own, let them feast. We march for the south and will deal with whoever they leave,' Inkark said.

Flames flew from Santra's hands as monsters emerged from the clouds. 'Carry nothing and run,' Avlor yelled running to retrieve two babes that had been sleeping in the back of a cart. As one of the fried monsters fell before Santra he saw the black shadows seeping over it and soon realised these creatures had once been falcons. Twisted they'd been by the shadows Inkark and his followers could now wield and this was but a glimpse of what the world would become under their Master's control. 'What are these things?' Elidom bellowed as a bright golden light covered him. All high elves have it in them to control the elements, Elidom though was blessed by Norcea herself and with that went the gift of her light. The light that went from his hands blinded the attacking creatures letting others flee, but more clouds covered the sky and Elidom's strength to hold back the darkness would soon fail. Falling to his knees Santra was quick to lift him to his feet and say. 'Hurry on with the others. I shall handle these.' The light around Elidom faded as his strength did, letting the creatures advance on the pair. 'I will not leave you to face this alone,' Elidom said, but flames already covered him. They didn't burn or harm him, but instead carried him from the clouds as the twisted falcons attacked. The fire faded and Elidom found himself at Martha's feet. Her child was soon thrust into his arms and she ordered him as if she were Norcea herself. 'Run Godborn, run and see he's safe. I must stand with him.' With a babe in each of Avlor's arms and another crying in Elidom's neither could follow as she ran to the mass of flames and shadows that battled. 'What do we do, Avlor? What do we do?' Elidom yelled with all the strength he could muster. Avlor though now saw black banners and the force Inkark had assembled in Duniesa draw close. Of all the possible futures that Avlor saw only one showed a path that would see the young in their care live. 'We have to leave it's the only way,' Avlor mumbled.

As the shadows surrounded Santra, talons and stabbing pecks cut through flames until he could stand no longer. Falling as Martha reached him creating a wall of mud and stone blocking the screeching monsters. 'You should have ran,' Santra cried. 'I could never run from you, Kuran is safe so with you I should be,' Martha told him as vines tore through their enemy. 'We will not survive this my love,' Santra whispered as they held each other close. 'I know, but together in the stars we will forever dwell,' Martha replied as their lips met and the wall she had created crumbled. Not broken by corrupt beasts, but shadows was her wall torn down by and passed it their wielder stood. It wasn't Inkark, but a shadow of him stood before them. From him darkness screamed and in their embrace both succumbed. Gone the Dune's were, but in the sky that night a new pair of lights shone. Two bright stars so close to one another they looked like one. Knocking three other stars aside to rest beside one another in the heavens forever more.

With the Lavender Lake in sight some hope returned to the World Builders, but this was quickly dashed as riders drew close. Handing one of the babes he carried to Elidom, Avlor placed a hand to the ground making roots run over the gorge before them to form a bridge. 'Hurry over,' he ordered as it reached the other side. 'Take the children and go with Avlor I shall hold them,' Elidom declared as more clouds followed the riders below. Corrupt falcons filled the sky above them and most feared they'd never make it over the long, unguarded bridge, but above the barren land of the south another's shadow now approached. For the master of the skies flew to their aid. The great griffin Charlemagne battled the demons in the sky as others below crossed to safety. Swooping down Charlemagne retrieved Elidom as Avlor made the bridge crumble so others couldn't follow. Landing on the south side Elidom thanked his old friend as another high elf approached. 'I warned you of this Elidom,' the brown cloaked man yelled to him. 'I warned you of Inkark's madness,' Edward Stanway said storming over. He was the Master of the Beasts and had left Duniesa many years hence, to roam and learn all he could of Alidor's beasts. Like the rest he had now been forced to flee by Inkark's forces. Screeching from above drew their eyes as more monsters darted around the sky, but the Master of the Beasts had long suspected the emergence of this dark magic. Using a broken branch as a staff he rose roots from the barren ground about them. 'Go Godborn, here is where this darkness stops,' he declared as the roots grew and turned white as they ascended. Joining together they became bark rising into the heavens to incredible heights. Casting out a bright light as it grew branches it parted the approaching clouds leaving the monstrous falcons to burn in its light. All others fled but Zolan and the other Builders stopped when they saw the tree growing. 'What is it?' Avlor asked. Seeing her stare in wonderment at the spectacle. 'No tree like that have I ever seen, even made by magic.'

'A Life Giver, your kind has surpassed all expectations. The same rests in Dunisea but far smaller she is. This one's roots will spread over the south and a new world will it create,' Zolan said. Their pursuers are for now halted while the Life Giver Edward created grew. It's light would hold back the darkness buying time for Elidom and his followers to reach a small patch of trees to the east. To the centre of these trees they went and there was the pod the Builders had spoken of. Within was all the Builders would need to rebuild, but so few they were. Only a handful had made the journey and most that were left had little will to go on. As she watched others enter the pod Elidom and Zolan both thought the same. 'We have only delayed the inevitable, they will soon find us,' Zolan said. 'Yes they will,' Avlor replied. 'They will find us, but you shall be protected when they do. I will see to that.'

'They're right,' Elidom said as he made a bed for the babes. 'You and I are all that's left Avlor, Inkark has won.'

'He has not won yet, for the beasts will fight for their lands,' Edward stated as he joined them. 'Let them come, I shall be ready but only won with might will this war be.' Rising before the others Avlor stated. 'War has come, we did not wish it and maybe through our desire to vie for peace we have emboldened our foes, but weak we are not. I can deal with this force he's created and the shadows he commands, but it is you who must end him Elidom.'

The light from the Life Giver did nothing to slow the riders leading Inkark's forces. A bridge was soon made and once over his force divided. Samuel and Famsa lead one to the patch of woodland the Builders hid within. While Inkark lead the rest to destroy the growing white bark tree. Alone Avlor now dug clay from the ground with his bare hands. Inside the pod the babies hid with the World Builders while he created their defenders. Using the clay he moulded what he would call a gargoyle. Once complete he placed his hand to the clay and passed a few years of his life over to it, bringing the lumps of clay into being. 'What's this all about then?' The gargoyle snapped as he looked around. 'You know your task yes?' Avlor asked.

'Task, what task? Just hungry I am and you look very tasty. Yes there's a lot of life left in you,' the gargoyle said. 'Don't worry many more like me are coming. Hurry into the woods and let none pass without feeding you,' Avlor said and on he went making as many as he was able each time giving over his own life to them. Leaving his skin wrinkled and his head balding as he lost hundreds of years of life. When the pair Inkark had sent lead their forces before the woodland the high elf's following them soon rushed in, but after they entered they quickly began to retreat. Forcing his soldiers on Samuel went beneath the trees followed by Famsa, but when they did both were thrown from their steeds. 'You must pay the toll,' a gargoyle declared as its claw's scratched at Samuel's face. Knocking the gargoyle away he ran from the trees. The menacing face of the gargoyle haunting him as he fled, leaving those who followed him at their mercy. Some High elves were drained of every ounce of their immortal life leaving just decaying corpses. While others who managed to flee the woodland like Famsa found themselves changed upon leaving the trees. Their ears had grown shorter and most found their control over the elements had gone. For the gargoyles had consumed all that Norcea once gifted them and no longer high elves were they. Elves is what they had become and the prey they had hunted now had a guard who would live on for years to protect them.

To the roots of the great tree Inkark's force marched and because of Tillamun's eyes they knew what waited before the white oak. It was a sight that had kept his eyes from straying. Beasts and titans of the forgotten age had assembled and leading them Elidom Godborn stood beside the master of the skies Charlemagne, along with the few high elves still loyal to him. 'Turn back,' Elidom declared. 'Turn back, let this war be done Inkark. Let it be just a blip in history. One that will soon be forgotten. For all our sakes turn back.'

'This war ends with your death Godborn and not until I see it and the last of the Builders fall dead at my feet will it be done. Norcea has forgotten you, she cares nothing for us so we shall make this world our own,' Inkark said. Rising his sword to the black clouds in the distance Elidom yelled back. 'You wish to live in darkness, to turn away from all we made bloom. Forget Norcea, forget gods and shadows we are brothers Inkark, let this end.'

'It will end, when the shadows rule all and the last light of Norcea fades,' Inkark announced and raised his hand as the light of the growing tree began to fade. It had reached its peak and as rain fell both forces advanced. Giants trampled high elves as other titans were brought down and hacked apart. Blood pooled around wolves and monsters from up high plucked beasts from the ground as war erupted in the south with a battle that saw few tactics or strategies. For neither side knew much of war, so savage the fighting was. Bodies and blood surrounded Elidom. Mud and sweat coated his face as his blade cut down others. The fading light in his hands guarded whoever he could as Inkark's forces encircled them and he saw their end near. Not yet though were those of the south defeated, for beneath the ground another titan dwelled. One who thought himself a god. To him the Master of the Beasts had gone and his pleas for aid had been heard. The ground cracked and from the depths of the earth goblins scurried to the surface in great numbers, swarming Inkark's forces. To Tillamun a group of goblins hurried and before he was able to flee he was pulled from his steed and stolen away. Not gold or riches had the Master of the Beasts promised the god of the underworld but a pair of eyes is what he offered, ones capable of foresight. Inkark's forces quickly fell to the swarm and as titans tore down who was left Inkark descended into madness. If not for Jandor ordering others to pull Inkark from the field he would have been taken up in the swarm of goblins. Dark clouds retreated and the sun shone once more but the goblin's aid came too late for many of the beasts and their Master wept for each. Walking the field nothing but death was about and just the Master of the Beast's wails could be heard as Elidom wiped blood from his eyes.

Days Inkark hoped it would take to return to the south, however once the truth of their failure was clear he realised it would take years for him to create an army capable of doing so. To Duniesa he retreated and once there he cursed all those he believed had failed him, sparing only Jandor for his loyalty. An easy feat given Tillamun had left behind the great tome he was gifted. Using it he sought out all of his former allies. Samuel had fled to the far south, but the shadows that had blessed them all allowed Inkark to reach them wherever they ran. To live only in the night and forever desire the blood of his own was the curse placed upon him. Tillamun was stolen from his captures by shadows before his eyes were taken and he was trapped in a realm of nightmares that lies between the world of the living and the dead. As for Famsa she had gone with others who'd changed at what became known as the Wanderer's Woods to live a relatively humble life. Until the day Inkark's shadows found her as she shopped for groceries. A darkness pooled about her feet, pulling her beneath the street of the town she'd fled to. Encaged under the streets forever more she would be forced to hear the minds of the hundreds that passed by.

Inkark however saw nothing amiss with his own actions so begged the god he served for more power to complete his work. Unfortunately this aid never came and after seven years his enemies had made plans of their own. In the dead of night Elidom snuck into Inkark's room and before his enemy could react he pierced his heart with his blade. Inkark though didn't die for the shadows would heal any wound he was dealt. So only to subdue him was this. Waking he noticed an elven woman grabbing his left hand while Avlor Tranem took his other. In unison they used the blades they held to cut his hands from his wrists. Inkark yelled as shadows tried to reform his hands, but both the woman and Avlor used fire to seal his wounds before they were able. Leaving Inkark with two charred black stumps where his hands used to be. Light then filled his eyes cast out from Elidom's hand, blinding him and stopping him from witnessing Jandor skulk away. The wretch had conspired with Elidom against Inkark to save his own wretched soul. Banished he then was to any land that would take him, but all he approached as he travelled only retched upon the sight of him. Passed the south he would go, to islands none yet knew of where he would plot a war of his own. Nothing but a lonely fool did Elidom take Jandor for, alike most who knew of him and without his eyes he believed him no threat. What he and no others knew is that as he fled Duniesa beneath his cloak he carried the black book both Tillamun and Inkark had been so taken with.

'Will that ensure his shadows can't heal him?' Elidom asked the woman who'd come with them. 'For a time we will need to keep him weak and fire to his wounds, once in Accultian we shall soon find a way to kill him,' the woman said. 'I have your word Godborn. You have your city, leave me free to experiment how I want in my fortress,' the woman said as others entered to carry Inkark to a waiting carriage. 'Yes. Do as you wish,' Elidom said his voice full of regret. Leaving the pair alone Avlor went to Elidom's side and asked. 'Can we trust this Countess?'

  'We have little choice, besides we cannot worry for her now there is much we must rebuild,' Elidom said. They looked over the city to see Inkark had done little to care for it or the people who followed him, but with him gone the light would slowly return to Duniesa. Guided them as the World Builders would have Avlor and Elidom did until Dunisea stood taller and grander than she ever had. The Seers they called them. The last of the first and Norcea's own light.

The First

Apprentice

Passed the wooden walls and great trees of Meceller the fields of Wearet lay. Here many towns and hamlets cover the vast swathes of land that is the Wearet. Green and fair this land is and the tall grass about it teemed with life, but that was before the humans began their purge. For now is the year six hundred and one and those of the Crown City along with their demon steeds plague the land. A few though were spared their wrath. Passed the walls of the forest city Meceller three brothers had rallied who they were able and set out to halt their enemy's advance. Rangers is what they called themselves. A name long lost to the wood folk after so many years relying on those in the golden tower to guard their safety. However, it is not with the three brothers where our story begins, but in a pool of blood drowning in sorrow do we find ourselves.

Fires burnt out while crows pecked at corpses and all around Fandisco Cariguan was death. The day had begun with such promise for none in the humble hamlet knew of what rode to them. Leaving them in blissful ignorance as many of the villagers rose with the sun and went into the streets. Tables and chairs were being set out for what the people of Floptins saw as the most important celebration of the year, the harvest festival. Nearly all the villagers were farmers or farm hands so once a year when the fields had been harvested and produce sold they joined together to eat, drink and be merry from morning to sunset. Unfortunately before cutlery could be placed upon the tables bells rang and the cries of anguish replaced the tranquil chirps of the crickets.

Pulling himself from the ruins of his family's home Fandisco wept as he fell. The blood soaked ground covered him as his hands landed in a puddle. The smell of charred and burning bodies made him gag. Retching he tried to cry, tried to scream out, but a small whine was all his scratching throat could muster. 'CAW look there,' a crow cried seeing him. 'They missed one CAW,' the crow went on. 'Not like them mutts to miss a tasty one like him CAW,' another cawed flapping into the air and landing closer to Fandisco. He though didn't hear or see them, trapped in his own woe he was. Even if the crows had flew over and plucked out his eyes in that moment he wouldn't have noticed. However as they approached an extremely unpleasant stink began to waft over the burning hamlet, a stink that soon made the crows fearful. 'CAW the rotter's here scarper, scarper,' one yelled. As a panic set in a couple of crows were in such a hurry to flee they crashed into others as they frantically flew away. The murder soon scattered leaving just the sound of fading fires to fill Floptins. Fandisco however didn't notice, to the pool of swirling red blood his eyes were fixed until not only his face looked back from the spinning reflection it created. The smell from the pipe the stranger had hanging from his mouth found him and his eyes rose to see a grumpy looking goblin. A black hooded cape covered him while beneath Fandisco could see many harnesses containing knives and daggers covering his grey tunic and trousers. The goblin aimed his long nose at the boy and said. 'What a sorry show this is,' with a sigh to Fandisco. 'I seek a Master Kanga little fellow, an imp or something or other I believe he is,' the goblin continued. Fandisco though just stared back with deep dead eyes until the wooden cane the goblin held began tapping him on the head. 'Well boy, do you know of him? Just my luck the greatest heist of my meagre life and I end up having to deal with the town numpty.'

'I don't know any Kanga,' Fandisco muttered as he felt his senses return. Blinking rapidly he noticed how irritated the goblin now looked. 'Blasted humans, blasted elves. How's a great thief meant to make his name with all this war.' Suddenly his eyes darted up and down Fandisco, quick as a flash he had dropped his cane and grabbed the boy by the collar, pulling him from the pool of blood and to his feet. 'Yes you may be just small enough, how old?' The goblin then snapped. 'Excuse me,' Fandisco asked.

'How old are you? Eleven or twelve I'd say,' the goblin replied.

'I'm twelve,' Fandisco said.

'Just as I said, I'd say you're skinny enough too,' the goblin went on retrieving his cane and tapping Fandisco's stomach with it. 'For what?' Fandisco asked getting increasingly worried as the goblin's gaze grew more intense by the second. 'For a heist boy. For the greatest heist this land has seen. Travel with me now, spend just a few days as my accomplice and by the end we will both have more wealth and fame than any thief that came before,' the goblin stated.

'Who, who are you? I'm no thief,' Fandisco stuttered. 'Not yet and after we part you need never be again. As for who I am, that is a tale I shall tell as we travel. If you dare to join me that is.' With that the goblin turned and began walking away leaving Fandisco stood before the ruins of his family home and the burnt corpses of his kin. A minute or so passed, but as the Rotting Thief had predicted footsteps soon hurried to his back. 'Wasiz,' the goblin yelled as Fandisco reached him. 'What's a Wasiz?' Fandisco replied.

'Me, I'm a Wasiz,' the goblin chuckled as they left Floptins.

On the pair went and because of Wasiz telling quite an elaborate tale regarding his dealings with the god of the underworld, it seemed to Fandisco at least to take even longer. Until he could finally take no more. Cutting in he said, 'Yes yes, you're so clever to outwit dwarves and gods as you did, but what is it you want to steal now? Where am I following you to?' Fandisco asked.

'Enough of that tone, you better learn a piece of respect if you're to be my apprentice,' Wasiz snapped back. 'I just wanted to leave there. Get away from that smell, I don't want to be your apprentice or anything like that,' Fandisco stated.

'Well when we find what we seek you will have the wealth to do whatever you please. For we go to find a double rainbow and the treasures it hides,' Wasiz told him.

'A double rainbow there's no such thing,' Fandisco argued. 'There most certainly is. I should know. Been tracking this one for half a year now, but the bugger who controls it knows of me and runs off hiding whenever I draw close. That's where you come in,' Wasiz said. Then he suddenly stopped talking as another's voice echoed around them. Light and fair the voice sounded and in a mocking tone it said. 'A goblin and an elf boy, funny pair aren't they brother. So far from the red water he is, while the north wonders why the young one left its safety.' Before Wasiz could speak Fandisco replied. The voice was so calming it put him instantly at ease, a feeling he'd all but forgotten until now. 'Never did I live in the north, from Floptins I am.' A figure then approached, hidden behind trees he had been, but this was not the owner of the mystery voice but it's brother. 'Spies I'd say they are, or smugglers perhaps, scoundrels for sure,' the other said striding before the pair. 'Especially this one,' he went on glaring at Wasiz. A green uniform he wore with a long sword on his belt and upon the breast pocket of his tunic the emblem of an oak leaf lay. 'Hurry now, name yourselves. The Crown marches and I have little time for fools.'

    'Fools he says, spies as well for we are just travelling. Rude is not a strong enough word for it, to ambush someone in such a way and berate them with questions. Whatever you call mother would be none too impressed with this I can tell you,' Wasiz said waving his cane about as he did. The sound of hooves then drew their attention to their backs. Both Fandisco and Wasiz span around to find a tall white horse and his rider had snuck behind them. 'Quite a skill that, to creep up on me,' Wasiz muttered to himself. 'He's right Richard we are being rude, tell him,' the rider said leaning forward on his saddle and looking down on the pair. 'Our family name is Balmoth, as he said I am Richard. There you have my brothers Jhona and Caspian, we are rangers,' Richard said with a huff.

'See, is having manners so hard. Be on your way now, no dealings with you rangers do we want,' Wasiz said.

'Answer us first who are you to be wandering around these lands freely while the human's wage war and why is the boy with you?' Jhona asked. 'Fandisco Cariguan is my name Sir and this here is Wasiz. I'm sorry about him,' Fandisco said still feeling charmed by Jhona's soft voice. 'And where is it you're going with him?' Jhona asked. 'To seek a double rainbow Sir,' Fandisco said as Wasiz's cane tapped him on the head once again. 'Enough of that,' Wasiz snapped.

'A double rainbow, of course you're here to steal something. Why else would a goblin be this far from the red water?' Richard said.

'It's a myth you know, a fable. There's no such thing,' Jhona stated.

'Exactly, the boy's just mad. Seen a lot back in Floptins he did. Now let us be on our way,' Wasiz ordered. 'Fine be off, we haven't the time for this. Wherever this rainbow is you seek I do hope it's further north. These lands will have few safe places by sunrise,' Richard said pushing Wasiz aside and going to his brothers. 'Which is why we can't just leave these two unaided,' Jhona replied climbing down from Caspian's back. 'You can't be serious,' Richard snapped.

'You and Caspian won't miss me for a day or two. I shall only see them to safety,' Jhona said. 'Listen to your brother we need no guard, best be on your way and find the rest of your rangers,' Wasiz said. 'I'm afraid my conscience just won't allow it. To leave you both wandering around war torn lands will have me constantly worrying. At least permit me to follow until I am sure this young man has found a safe place,' Jhona insisted.

'Of course you can join us Sir,' Fandisco said. Jumping to Jhona's side and taking his hand, extremely excited he may be accompanying them. 'There is no need,' Wasiz protested once again, but the others made it clear the decision had been made. While Caspian and Richard rode on to find the rest of the rangers, Jhona kept hold of Fandisco's hand and followed Wasiz while he muttered and moaned to himself.

The path they followed took them from the fields of the Wearet, west over the Arizun steam and then back into a nest of birch trees. From there though Wasiz seemed to get rather puzzled when the path split. 'West or south, oh what was it? Think, think,' he muttered while scratching his head. 'What's the matter?' Fandisco asked.

'He's lost,' Jhona mocked.

'Am not,' Wasiz snapped. 'I just need to get my bearings is all.' He carried on grumbling to himself while his companions folded their arms and began tapping their toes, both getting quite tired of waiting. 'Blast it we shall just have to wait until sunrise to see the path,' Wasiz said.

'So you are lost?' Jhona said.

'We are not lost, only slightly delayed. Feel free to run along back to your rangers if you perceive us to be taking up too much of your valuable time,' Wasiz replied.

'Don't worry yourself, my brothers are quite capable. I have an abundance of hours to spare,' Jhona smirked with a mocking grin over his face making the grumbly goblin even more so. 'If you don't mind, I'm quite hungry. If we are stopping, would I be able to get something to eat,' Fandisco asked. While Jhona had been enjoying watching Wasiz pacing back and forth with his frustration growing, Fandisco had been more focused on his growling belly. 'Is he yet to even feed you? It's decided then, my brothers and I have passed this way a few times. Come along I should be able to find our last camp,' Jhona said. A little off the road and through drooping ferns they went until Jhona stopped where a fallen log sat before a ring of stones. Both he and Fandisco set about making a fire while Wasiz continued to groan to himself as he scratched his head and puffed on his pipe. With the fire lit Jhona went into his pack and removed a loaf of bread and a bag of beans. 'A meagre meal I'm afraid,' he said finding a bowl for the beans from his pack and placing the bread over the fire. 'No it's more than I expected Sir,' Fandisco replied even more eager to eat than he realised. 'Enough of that Sir stuff, it hardy suits me. Here,' Jhona said handing a large oak leaf to Fandisco that contained two slices of perfectly toasted bread covered in beans. 'Thank you, I'll see if Wasiz wants any,' Fandisco said but when he stood up he noticed the goblin had vanished. 'Where has he ran off to?'

'I shouldn't worry for him,' Jhona told him. 'Do you think he's coming back?' Fandisco asked sitting back down at the fire. 'I'm sure he will be. Enough about the thief though, what of you? Most elves I know make a point of staying north of the Lavender Lake, even before the war. What brought you this far south?' Jhona asked.

'My father was a trader, just fruit and vegetables, nothing too taxing is what he would say. A couple of years after he visited Floptins he came home raving about the place and the people. Said he'd had enough of the city and before my mother knew it he had sold his business and they were moving there. It was meant to be perfect he said it would be anyhow, but then the war started and everything changed,' Fandisco trailed off into silence until he was staring into his dinner. 'How did the thief find you?' Jhona asked.

'Everyone was happy, nothing was amiss, then the fires started and everyone began yelling. The howls followed soon after and my mother rushed me into the cellar. She went back for my brother but...' As it all came flooding back

Fandisco's hands shook so hard he dropped his food. His eyes filled with tears and he found Jhona's arms around him. 'Hush, far from any of that you are now,' he said, but before he could comfort the boy more Wasiz burst through the bushes. 'Time to go,' he said rushing passed the pair. 'What's going on?' Jhona yelled after him but got his answer from the groans that were following him. 'A rinasore. How did you upset a rinasore?' Jhona yelled quickly grabbing his pack along with Fandisco's hand and running after the Rotting Thief as the rinasore ripped through the bushes after them. 'What did you do?' Jhona shouted again when he reached Wasiz. Over three meters tall and wider than two ample carriages beside one another this beast is. With four tremendous horns along its lower jaw and another that splits into two spears at the end of its snout. 'I was just having a stroll and he took offence,' Wasiz replied.

'Unlikely, they're as passive as they get,' Jhona said. 'Well this one clearly isn't,' Wasiz shouted back as they retreated from the trees and onto the road. 'Sod it, south. We go south.'

'Have you remembered the way?' Fandisco asked. 'Whatever way will do now,' Wasiz said grabbing Fandisco around the waist and lifting him up onto his back. He turned out to be surprisingly spritely with a rinasore behind him, after appearing so aged during their journey thus far.

An hour of frantic running followed until Jhona finally said. 'That's it, I think it's given up,' Fandisco climbed down from Wasiz's back as the others began panting, both almost falling to the floor from exhaustion. 'Where are they?'

'Where's what?' Wasiz asked.

'The beast's eggs. A rinasore wouldn't chase us this far without a reason,' Jhona said.

'I don't know what you mean,' Wasiz responded holding tight to the bag he had over his shoulder. In a flash Jhona was ontop of him and soon had the bag from his grasp, but to his surprise it didn't contain any eggs. 'Where are they?'

'I swear I didn't take anything, but if I knew I'd get this sort of treatment for it I'd have done it a lot sooner,' Wasiz joked with a bent grin up to Jhona. 'When you two are finished, do you want to see if that's the rainbow you're after?' Fandisco said pointing to the sun rising on the horizon slowly illuminating the glimmering colours of a rainbow. 'That's the one, told you it was south,' Wasiz said as Jhona leapt up.

'You had no idea what way it was,' Fandisco reminded him.

'Never mind that,' Wasiz said pushing passed him. 'Looks like a regular rainbow to me,' Jhona commented. 'Use them fancy woody eyes of yours and look closer. There see, hidden in its glow is the second, but only one end touches the ground. That's where our treasure is hidden,' Wasiz claimed. 'If you say so,' Jhona huffed.

'I do and I'm afraid this is where we must leave our young charge,' Wasiz said. 'If I go any further he will surely notice me, and a ranger will certainly draw his eye.'

'He's only joking there's still miles to go,' Fandisco said to Jhona hoping he was right. 'No joke lad, but don't fear just follow the second rainbow to where it meets the ground. There you should find a tunnel, at the end of it is the prize we seek,' Wasiz said. Going into his bag he revealed a rusty key. The teeth of the key were odd shapes and the end had been twisted into a skull. 'Here this will open whatever may be holding it.'

'That can't be all you're giving him,' Jhona said. 'He shouldn't need anything more, if he's smart that is,' Wasiz replied.

'Here take this also, the dagger is weak but is made from refined werinder bark and once drawn will sing. If you get into trouble wield it and I will hear and come running,' Jhona said taking a sheathed dagger from his belt and tying it to Fandisco's. 'On your way now, be off before the sun moves and hides it once again,' Wasiz insisted ushering him on. Strangely enough Fandisco didn't feel nervous or even worried about what he may find and went forth with quite a spring in his step. Jhona however was grateful to finally have time to question the thief without his young charge hearing. 'So why him?' Jhona asked the second Fandisco was out of earshot. 'You know more of me than I feel you have said,' Wasiz replied.

'I may have heard a tale or two. That is why I wonder what the Rotting Thief needs a child's aid for,' Jhona said.

'He got lucky,' Wasiz told him. 'I was just passing and there he was covered in blood, lost beyond care. So I begged him to aid me purely to take him from there and save him from the crows,'

Wasiz said. 'Seems you have more compassion than you show Rotting Thief,' Jhona giggled unable to help himself growing fonder of the rogue. 'My dear Jhona there's plenty of me you are yet to see and a few more tales you're yet to hear,' Wasiz replied raising his eyebrows with a cunning grin.

It didn't take long for Fandisco's worry to creep back after he left the others, but with his hand to the dagger on his belt he found the confidence to carry on. Though he began to realise he was more anxious to discover what the second rainbow hid than he'd expected. *Maybe it's shiny red diamonds or emeralds perhaps, but what if it's just a pile of gold how will I carry it all out* he wondered, but had to stop wondering when he noticed how close to the first rainbow he'd already gotten. What young Fandisco didn't know was that this rainbow was following him in a desperate attempt to draw his eyes from the second, but unlike most who pass it by Fandisco knew that the second fainter rainbow hid the real prize. Once he passed by the other and after its glow didn't obscure his view he could see that around half a mile south west the second rainbow appeared to meet the ground. Drawing closer Fandisco saw its faint glimmer on the top of a grassy mound. *Well this is definitely where it ends, but I don't see any tunnel or treasure like Wasiz said.* Going into the fading rainbow he became surrounded by the many colours, raising his arm he noticed colourful sparks landing on him. A red spark was first, followed by violet, then yellow until all the colours of the rainbow covered him. All of a sudden the sparks leapt from him and before Fandisco could react the ground beneath his feet fell away. Dropping him into the lair he was sent to steal from.

The hole Fandisco fell through resealed itself as quickly as it opened. Making our young thief's hand instantly reach for the werinder bark dagger. Blinking rapidly Fandisco forced his eyes to adjust to the darkness and when they finally did he was surprised by what he saw. Instead of a dark horror infested passage he found green and purple mushrooms covering the walls and floor. Running along the many roots that cascaded down the wall small luminous bulbs gave off just enough light to make it feel warm. Relaxing but only slightly given the situation, Fandisco timidly went on. The path before him grew larger until it split at a cross roads going in four directions. *Trust Wasiz to say nothing about this.* Seeing no other choice and not wanting to get lost in whatever darkness lay beyond, Fandisco reached for the dagger Jhona had given him. Before he could draw it a voice stopped him, coming down from one of the tunnels on the left it was. Running to the wall Fandisco found a small nook to conceal himself within. 'Whose that blasted rainbow let in now? Does whatever it pleases that thing does.' Fandisco heard someone say as the voice approached. Slurred and bitter was his voice. 'It's not its fault, you're too harsh on it you are.' Another voice that went with the other said. 'It needs feeding, probably just hungry. I bet it is.' The other's voice sounded a tad sweeter but just as guttural as the first. Concealed Fandisco was as a torch drew close and then stopped. 'Shut it,' the bitter voice yelled followed by a yelp from the other as if he'd been hit. Looking out Fandisco saw the owners of this lair bickering before him. Now most, mainly those in the north believe leprechauns to be charming little folk with bushy beards and oversized green hats, but in truth there is nothing charming about them as Fandisco saw. His gaze went up the leprechaun from its blue grey feet with its overgrown and broken nails, passed its thin chicken like legs to his wasted torso covered in rotten cloth. Skipping his gangly arms and twisted fingers Fandisco's eyes then noticed his two heads. 'But, but,' the head wearing a faded flat cap said. 'Shut it, or another slap you'll get.' The other head that wore a torn top hat spat. 'I ain't feeding that thing until it works right. I'd not feed you if I didn't have to. Move that sodding leg and let's sort it,' he ordered threatening the other. The torch light faded as the leprechaun went down another tunnel and Fandisco crept out with a plan in mind. *Whatever the it is they're on about must be what Wasiz is after.* So with his hand firmly to the handle of his dagger he followed the torch light at a safe distance, until more lights joined it and Fandisco found himself in a small cave. Covered in the same mushrooms and bulbs as the tunnel it was and to the centre the leprechaun went where a small metal cage sat. Picking it up with his left arm and violently shaking the cage the one wearing the top hat yelled. 'Who'd you let in? Where are they?' Barely audible terrified squeaks came from within the cage. 'Blasted damn useless thing.' Tossing the cage down the leprechaun stormed off shouting. 'I'll get the poker, see if its this much trouble after that.' Once away Fandisco snuck over to the cage and found it contained a little round furry yellow ball. 'Well what sort of treasure is this meant to be,' Fandisco said causing a pair of white eyes with tiny black pupils to open in the middle of the ball. Suddenly it began to squeak in a panic. 'Calm down whatever you are, here let's get you out of there,' Fandisco said. Taking the key Wasiz gave him from his pocket it began to change shape to fit the lock, until it clicked and the door of the box flung open letting the little furry thing hop free. 'Come on, I can't imagine that thing has anything else of worth around here.' The fluffy thing then hopped away from Fandisco to a backpack that was sat upon one of the larger mushrooms. Looking in he saw it contained a folded up piece of blank parchment. Jumping up and down the fluffy thing clearly wanted Fandisco to take it, so he put it in his back pocket. Taking the fluffy thing in his hand he went back the way he came, but not many steps did he take before his thieving was noticed. 'See I told ya,' Fandisco heard the rage filled voice cry out. 'I told ya, it let one in. I told ya it did.' Quickening his pace as he heard the yells draw closer. Fandisco was sure he could out run the leprechaun, but how would he open the ground to get out. Before he could worry more he heard the leprechaun scream. 'There it is, there's the tea leaf.' Swinging the red hot poker he wielded he sliced Fandisco across the back of his legs knocking him to the floor leaving the fluffy thing to jump up to his defence. 'Don't, I'm sure he didn't mean to.' The other head said using his right arm to stop the other swinging. 'Get off, I said its for a poking didn't I.' The one in the top hat screamed as he batted away the other, buying Fandisco mere seconds to draw the werinder dagger. The sound it emitted was like a melody to Fandisco but from the high pitched wails coming from the leprechaun Fandisco imagined it must have sounded awful to them. 'Do you wish it to stop? Well do you?' Fandisco said forcing himself to his feet and waving the dagger before them. 'Yes, yes make it stop. Please.' The one in the flat cap spluttered. 'Horrible, nasty elfie noise stop it, stop.' The other yelled dropping his poker to cover his ear. 'I'll make it stop but only once I'm free of here. Show me the way out and you shall never hear it again,' Fandisco ordered.

'Yes, yes,' the kinder head said.

'No, he's a thief. He's tricking us,' the meaner butted in letting go of his ear to reach for his poker, but the sound was unbearable and his hand was soon back over his ear. 'Fine, but the Fluttylin stays.'

'The what?' Fandisco asked.

'That thing,' the leprechaun replied using his elbow to gesture to the fluffy thing. 'No, he's coming with me,' Fandisco said turning to see the Fluttylin had been controlling the rainbow and now used it to open an exit above their heads. 'Seems we no longer need to make a deal,' Fandisco declared as the leprechaun fell to its knees. Running to the opening Fandisco stabbed the dagger into the wall. After picking up the Fluttylin Fandisco climbed out of the hole, leaving the leprechaun trapped beneath the ground. In agony it slowly crawled over the floor to try and break the dagger and end the cursed song that now rang in his ears.

Once through the hole was quickly closed behind Fandisco sealing away the leprechaun's lair. After it shut the second rainbow soon vanished leaving the other to fade in the sun. 'I see why Wasiz thinks you're some special treasure now,' Fandisco said as the fluttylin joyfully hopped beside him. 'I wonder where they are, Jhona said he'd hear if I used the dagger.' As Fandisco picked himself up a worrying sight found him. Only twenty feet away a huge wolf with bloody jaws stood. Feasting on a slain boar he was, but now two tastier morsels had just crawled out of the ground begging to be eaten. Leaping from his meal it bounded towards Fandisco. Rising up before him the beast's jaws flicked vile over his face. Then suddenly it was before Fandisco's feet, dead. A long dagger had pierced its neck and before Fandisco could think he was flung up and found himself on Caspian's back. 'Go Caspian, return to Richard and tell him Gustom's forces have outflanked us,' Jhona said. After a nod to Fandisco he took the bow and arrows from Caspian's saddle as howls drew close. 'What's happening? I got your treasure,' Fandisco said seeing Wasiz before him. His cape had fallen away and instead of a hunched over old goblin he now looked like a young warrior. Two swords he held in one hand while the other wielded a series of throwing knives. The howls stopped and upon the peak of the hill before them a human clad in black armour astride a grey steel covered wolf yelled down to them. 'Surrender Balmoth and your death will be quick,' Gustom Chiris announced. Leader of the infamous Sainted Scouts, formed by King Harold Hargo to go ahead of his full force. To sabotage and waylay enemy marches was their job, but with a force of two hundred men and wolves to his back Gustom had branched out as a barbarian, raiding and pillaging the lands of the Wearet freely until the Balmoths and their rangers joined the fray. 'What of me wolf man?' Wasiz yelled up. 'What fate would befall a great thief such as I?'

'I don't know you worm, leave here with your life,' Gustom replied.

'You best do Wasiz, take Fandisco and get clear of here,' Jhona said as more riders joined Gustom, but Wasiz didn't hear a word of it. 'Haven't heard, you haven't heard. Do you sleep under rocks with that mutt sat on your face? For only the dim do not know of the Rotting Thief,' Wasiz bellowed seemingly more concerned for his reputation than the danger before them. 'Feast on the other but I want the Balmoth,' Gustom cried and with great howls the wolves ran to them. 'Run Caspian,' Jhona ordered and reluctantly he did. Charging away on Caspian's back Fandisco watched the wolves rushing to the others. He tried to keep hold of the fluttylin but it wriggled free from his hand, jumping to the ground. 'Stop Caspian, I dropped him,' Fandisco said making Caspian turn back to see the fluttylin hopping up and down changing colour rapidly as he did. Fandisco leapt off Caspian and went to run to it but the steed's neighs made him stop.

With every arrow Jhona fired another wolf or their rider fell, but both he and the Rotting Thief would soon be overwhelmed in the charging mass of fangs and steel. 'Why did you stay you fool?' Jhona said. 'Better a remembered fool than a forgotten hero my dear Jhona,' Wasiz replied throwing multiple daggers to the necks of riders.

Black clouds then filled the sky above the pair as their enemy encircled them. Rain began to fall but before even one drop touched the ground lightening struck the earth around the wolves. 'What is this?' Jhona yelled as the rain poured and lightening scarred the land about them. 'It's you doing it, isn't it?' Fandisco shouted to the fluttylin. Jumping up he punched into the air and shouted as thunder rocked the sky. 'That's it you fluffy little master of the weather,' The fluttylin could only do so much though and the dark clouds soon faded. 'No, no you can't stop yet, they're still coming,' Fandisco said picking the fluttylin up. 'The poor thing's exhausted let it rest, we can handle the rest,' a familiar voice said making Fandisco spin. 'Richard,' Fandisco said as the ranger pulled himself onto Caspian's back. 'Thank you for guarding my brother for me young thief, maybe a Ranger's uniform would suit you better than a thief's cowl. Later for that however, for now the rangers must ride,' Richard stated. Drawing his sword Caspian rose up and with a war cry from each they charged. More hooves followed forcing Fandisco to climb a tree to avoid being trampled by the hundreds of hooves charging passed him into battle. Gustom's fall was the reformed rangers first true victory over the armies of the Crown City, but even with the aid of the fluttylin it was a hard fought battle. A force of more than ninety rangers and their steeds quickly fell to under thirty. Bloody and brutal was this battle one Fandisco found himself unable to even watch, for the sight of a wolf tearing a body apart is one best left unseen. A knife to the throat of Gustom's wolf ended the beast and soon after his master's head was hewed by Richard's blade. Seeing the last of the wolves flee Fandisco ran down to them. Passed the dead and dying he went until his arms found Jhona. Fandisco found him kneeling on the ground, he was exhausted. His bow was broken, his uniform torn, but Fandisco only saw that he was alive. 'Ah there you are, well where's my treasure?' Wasiz said strolling over.

'You really still care about that,' Fandisco said. 'Of course I do, I would not have ended up in this mess if not for it,' Wasiz replied.

'Here,' Fandisco stated holding out his hands and showing Wasiz the fluttylin. 'What's that?' Wasiz asked.

'It's a fluttylin. They can control the weather,' Jhona told them. 'Guess it's you we have to thank for delaying their charge.'

'What? That's not it. Where's the rest?' Wasiz said spinning Fandisco around and searching his pockets. 'Good work lad, good work,' he went on after retrieving the blank parchment. 'Why did you want a bit of paper so much?' Jhona asked. Pulling him and Fandisco close so others couldn't hear Wasiz said. 'Because this paper will lead to even greater treasures. A map it is, one that will find any path even those of legend.'

'Wait so I have to do more thieving to get paid,' Fandisco said. Starting to get quite annoyed not to be getting paid immediately after all the effort he'd put in. 'Do not fret if you wish you can head on with Jhona and a fine ranger I'm sure you'll be. A man of my word am I so by this time next year I will return with the wealth I promised you,' Wasiz said as a joy filled smile began creeping over his face making it clear he was thinking of the heists to come. With the waft of his cape he concealed himself beneath it once again and began to walk away. *That's that then* Fandisco thought until Jhona said. 'You know the life of a ranger is a hard one. Harder though is the life of a thief and few ever get the chance to be a good one. A ranger I see in you, but only a handful I feel will ever get the chance to learn his ways.'

'You're telling me to follow him,' Fandisco said. 'I'm telling you to choose for yourself young master. Rarely is the path clear to follow but it is you who must decide which direction it goes,' Jhona said. He then went to rejoin his brothers. For a minute Fandisco stayed still, wondering what to do. Then seeing Jhona surrounded by family and Wasiz with none he quickly made his choice. 'So where is first on this magic map?' Fandisco asked rejoining Wasiz with the fluttylin on his shoulder. 'What do you know about pankor taming?' Wasiz asked. 'What, I don't know anything about it, why would I? Who would even want to tame a Pankor?' Fandisco replied. 'Well you better start learning, seems we're heading to the circus,' Wasiz grinned showing Fandisco the red and white tent that had appeared on the stolen map.

A
Forgettable
Feather

'It's called a shining hoopoe,' Franklin Toffen said as he slid a book about the bird over the table to Makron La Sore. 'My father told me of them when I was young, but said they were just a story,' Brendan Caster interjected. The three of them sat at the Elite's table in the centre of the Ranger's Academy's great hall and spoke as the hall filled with other students for that evening's dinner. 'It's not just a story. I was speaking to that chap who brings the groceries. He said one was seen just a mile east of here. If we could just pluck one feather from it we'd be able to prove they're real. We'd all go home to Dunisea famous if we did and have our pick of posts when we graduate,' Franklin insisted. 'A mile east of here is the Glade, there's only sparrows flying about those trees,' Brendan argued. 'Then it won't hurt sneaking out tonight to go take a look will it,' Franklin said as Makron noticed another student heading to the Ranger's table. Waving to him Makron shouted over. 'Think Jenna can still keep pace with Chaplin?'

'From what I remember it was the pair of you falling behind last time we rode together,' James Balmoth said sitting on the opposite side of the table to Makron. Looking over them James noticed Franklin trying to hide a page on the open book before him. 'What are you up to?'

'Never you mind Balmoth, nothing you Rangers would be interested in. This is Elite business,' Franklin snapped back.

'Don't be stubborn,' Makron said. 'How would you feel about a field trip tonight?'

'We don't need him,' Franklin argued.

'Do either of you have a horse?' Makron asked knowing neither Franklin or Brendan did, causing both to fall silent. 'It's settled then, we can sneak out once everyone else has gone to bed.' With that James was informed about the shining hoopoe and they agreed to meet at the stables once the rest of the academy had gone to sleep.

'Quickly get in,' Brendan ordered pushing Makron and Franklin behind the stable door. 'What took you so long? I have Jenna and Chaplin ready to go,' James said referring to the pair of horses behind him, before he was pushed behind the door also. 'Professor Carny's trotting about,' Brendan said as he shoved James into Makron's side. Beyond the door the old centaur patrolled the grounds carrying a flickering lantern, aiming to scupper the plans of any students who wished to cause trouble. 'He's heading away, I don't think he saw us,' Franklin said.

'Good, last thing we need is that old grump scolding us. I'll go with James, you two take Chaplin,' Makron ordered as Brendan retrieved three swords he had hidden under a hay bale earlier that day. 'Sorry James I could only get three,' Brendan said.

'Don't worry, I only need my bow,' James replied. Taking the steeds from the stables they snuck with them to the academy's gates. There they climbed into the saddles and headed to the Glade. A journey that would normally have been a fairly easy ride over flat ground, but with both Jenna and Chaplin competing to out match one another all were quite shaken up when they arrived. 'My back's killing me,' Brendan complained as he climbed from Chaplin's saddle. 'They didn't slow down once after we got clear of the academy, never seen Chaplin so wound up.' Taking an apple from Chaplin's saddle bag Makron fed it to him. 'He's worn himself out trying to keep up with Jenna. You hear that, you'll have to take it easy on the way back. You're getting too old to keep racing her,' Makron said. Chaplin shook his mane as he munched on the apple, causing the juice to spray over Makron as he did. 'I told you, even other Meceller horses can barely keep up with her. They can rest here while we go on,' James said taking his bow from Jenna's saddle. 'Hurry up we don't have all night,' Franklin said running beneath the trees of the woods. 'Don't rush off you'll get lost,' Brendan yelled going after him forcing Makron and James to follow.

The full moon let beams of its light cut through gaps in the treetops lighting the way for the four of them. Pink petals fell around from blossoming crab apple trees and would have made their stroll a quite charming endeavour, slightly romantic even if not for Franklin that is. Every tree or bush they passed he would dive into or try to climb in a attempt to locate the shining hoopoe's nest. Sadly after finding nothing and searching for more than an hour both Brendan and Franklin were getting rather frustrated. James and Makron on the other hand had both been happy to just walk along the path together, walking so close that almost every step they took caused their arms to brush against one another. Both seemed to forget the others were there until Franklin jumped out before them. 'Stop falling behind to flirt with your woody and help,' he said to Makron as he walked backwards down the path. 'We weren't,' James blushed.

'You're the hoopoe expert what help could we be anyway,' Makron joked.

'It must be around here somewhere, do you not know any woody tricks that will draw it out?' Franklin asked James. 'None that I know,' James laughed as Franklin tripped and fell back on what he thought was a fallen branch. 'Don't move,' Brendan whispered as the branch slowly retreated into a bush letting out a groan from within as it went. 'What is it?' Franklin said as the bush began to rise before them. As dead leaves and bracken fell away they saw it was no branch, but a brown fur covered leg with five large toes whose claws scratched the ground as it went. Suddenly eyes and a feline face emerged from the bush as the creature pulled its body from under the soil it had been concealed by. 'It's a bush pankor just stay still, it

will move on when it sees we aren't a threat,'
Brendan said. With all four of its paws pulled from
under the ground the pankor let out a spine tingling
roar that made Franklin's terrified legs act on
instinct. Turning to run away Franklin heard the
pankor breaking bracken as it pounced and before
he knew what was happening he had been thrown
through the air. Smashing to the floor the pankor's
black teeth were soon before Franklin. An
extremely irritated look then shot across the
pankor's face and the creature turned to see
Makron and Brendan pulling on its tail, attempting
to pull it away from Franklin. Only a slight
annoyance to the pankor the pair were. With one
mighty flick of his tail both of them were thrown
down and the pankor's drooling mouth turned back
to Franklin. However for a second time before it
could act the pankor's face changed again, this
time though he looked far from annoyed. Whilst
his friends looked on and Franklin scurried back to
the others James sang. Singing a song the pankor
appeared quite taken by. 'So glad I was to find
your frown, I do so love to endeavour to turn it
around. My love I found with just a smile, one
rarely seen for quite awhile. Thrilled I was to act

the fool until your frown broke and beat away your gloom. Hardly a second can pass without it haunting me, your grin, your laugh, your blushing red cheeks. All fills every minute, every second of each waking day and when I sleep all I see is your face. So long has now passed since I saw it last, still it's clear your smile to me but longing am I to find it once more so much so I wish to run to your door.' As James' song came to an end the pankor looked completely at ease and if you were to listen closely you'd even have heard a slight purr coming from him. Contented none around meant him any harm the pankor strolled back to where he was sleeping, his bushy mane still swaying to the melody. 'How did you know singing would work?' Brendan asked. 'And how do you know such a soppy song?' Franklin added as he wiped pankor saliva from his jacket. 'My mother told me a story about how a shepherd would keep them from his sheep by singing them songs. To be honest I'm as amazed as you it worked,' James said looking to the pankor who was busy reburying his bottom half. 'Did she tell you the song also?' Brendan asked. 'No, a friend taught it to me,' James replied.

'Come along then,' Franklin said. 'This bird won't pluck itself.'

'You can't still want to keep searching,' Makron snapped. 'I'm not coming all this way and going back with nothing. Just one more hour,' Franklin insisted as he grabbed Brendan and dragged him on with him. Taking James' arm before he could follow Makron said. 'Fine, but we're done walking around. The pair of us will wait here and come save you when you upset another beast,' Makron said. After their friends disappeared passed trees Makron spun James to face him and put his arms around him, like the pair were about to dance. 'Stop it they'll see,' James said but in truth he did nothing to remove Makron's arms. 'Let them, for I only agreed to come tonight to be close to you,' Makron said.

'You don't mean that,' James replied.

'I do. Let them see and let us be free from having to hide,' Makron said.

'It's not them I worry for, it's who they will tell,' James told him.

'My father can't control me forever James, already Vanessa pulls away from him. Once she's old enough together we will make our mother see sense. Whatever spell he has her under can be broken. I'm sure of it,' Makron insisted as James head rested on his chest. 'You don't know that, not for sure,' James said. 'I wont let you give him an excuse to harm you in any way, especially if it's just for my sake.'

'It's for all our sakes James. Not just you and I, but my sister and mother also. It's funny though, I was certain you'd forgotten our song,' Makron said. 'I still carry it,' James replied hiding his face out of embarrassment. 'You don't really, do you?' Makron asked. Leaning back James unbuttoned the top pocket of his jacket to reveal the letter Makron had written him a couple of years ago. 'You're far more sentimental than I realised Balmoth,' Makron teased as he pushed James back so he had his back up against a tree. Going close both grew goosebumps over their arms as their lips inched closer, but a loud squawk from above their heads stopped them both. Looking up they saw perched on a branch above them the shining hoopoe sat.

'Does this mean we need to call the others back?' Makron said. 'We probably should,' James sighed.

'What you two doing on my tree?' The annoyed shining hoopoe squawked down. 'Don't be mucking it up, just got it all how I like it I have.'

'Brilliant, it can talk,' Makron scoffed.

'Course I can talk, how else would I stop pests mucking up my tree,' the hoopoe said.

'You found it, you really found it,' Franklin yelled running back over with Brendan. 'Great more ruffians. I'll see about you lot I will. Kyir get over here and eat this lot,' the hoopoe said shouting over to the bush pankor, but only a huff came from him. 'Damn useless kitten, ask you to guard my nest and all you do is sleep.' The hoopoe's complaining went on until James said. 'We are sorry to have intruded on your tree and a very nice one it is. All we seek is a feather if you have one to spare.'

'And what would you do with it?' The hoopoe asked. 'Many come looking for my kin, most were found and once so their trees soon fall. Elves care little for beasts and birds, not like the first are they.' Flapping its wings the hoopoe flew down to a lower branch. 'I promise you none of us wish to cut down your tree, only to prove your kind still exist is why we want one,' Franklin insisted. Looking over the group the hoopoe then said. 'A strange company this is, a high elf and wood folk, two elves also. Perhaps a little of the first goes with you and there's some sense amongst you. After a minute or two more of grumbling the hoopoe announced. 'So be it, if it will get you away.' Jumping from the branch the hoopoe flew to the top of the tree where his nest sat. Remerging from the leafy treetop he fluttered back down with a perfectly preserved feather in between his beak. 'Here,' the hoopoe said and held it out to Franklin. 'Take it and be off with you, but don't be sending others back here to muck up my tree. That useless cat might actually eat them.'

'You have a deal, does he not Franklin?' Makron said. 'What, oh yes yes, I suppose he does,' Franklin replied.

'Come on we're going to have to rush to get back before daylight,' Brendan told them.

'Yes, get off with you,' the hoopoe ordered as he took himself back to bed.

The four of them made their way back to where the horses waited and as they went each wondered about what the shining hoopoe had said. All save for Franklin that is, who was far too busy admiring his prize. 'He was right you know, if you take that back to Duniesa, even if you just show it off at the academy others will flock here looking for one of their own,' Makron said.

'Nice to hear you speaking sense for once,' James joked. 'I do agree though both he and that pankor are perfectly happy without a stream of people walking through their woods.'

'So what, we just leave it?' Franklin said.

'If we don't this place will turn into a fairground, our fathers alone would send all their yuppie friends here and that would just be the start of it. All they have to worry for at the moment is the odd grocer's rumour and the ones foolish enough to believe them,' Brendan added.

'Someone will come along and find them soon enough, why should we not be the one gaining the fame from it?' Franklin argued.

'Maybe someone will, but at least it won't be us that ruin this place. Who knows they may come to the same decision as us,' Makron said.

'No one said we'd made a decision,' Franklin stated. 'Stop being stubborn you know it's the right thing to do,' Brendan said.

'I suppose so,' Franklin sighed. 'I'm burying it though.' Removing the sword from his belt he began to dig a hole in the mud to hide the feather in. 'Just put it under some leaves,' Brendan said. 'No way,' Franklin snapped 'I don't want that grocer turning up in a week boasting he found it just sat by the road. If anyone else wants one they'll have to face off against a bush pankor, same as we did.'

Going at a slightly less brisk pace meant the sun was already beginning to rise when they snuck back through the gates of the Ranger's Academy. Leaving Jenna and Chaplin to take themselves back to the stables the boys hurried to their dorms. 'You know it's not like we're going to get much sleep now, you may as well come back to the Elite's dorm with us James. I have some delicious stollen bread my mother sent me. There's enough sugar filled marzipan on it to keep us awake for the rest of the day,' Franklin said as they went. Returning to the window they originally snuck out of Brendan climbed through, followed closely by Makron and Franklin. Unfortunately the barrel they were using as a step up gave way when James stood on it. Sending him tumbling back and rolling over the ground, leaving him beneath the windows of the home economic's dorm that lay opposite, just as Professor Carny walked by. Leaving the others hiding under the window James was marched off to the Headmistress's office. Even after a lengthy interrogation by the Headmistress and a suspension neither James or anyone else ever spoke of the shining hoopoe or its feather to another.

When

The

Shadows

Returned

None strike fear like those of the Blood Works. None are as mighty or as savage as they. From birth the orcs of this dreaded isle are trained. Taken from the arms of their mothers and examined they are, by the Keeper of the Ways. A particularly cruel orc the Keeper is and diligently he acts out his ways however he sees fit. Checking each child for any deformities or misshapen limbs. If even the slightest imperfection was found the babes were discarded and cast from Gropas Falls, to be consumed by the raging sea below. The threat of death would still remain over all those who passed this trial and the many others the Keeper of the Ways would make them suffer through. For one misstep, one dropped cup or blunted blade could lead the Keeper to see one as feeble. In his wicked eyes a feeble orc is of no use to the horde, so cast down these were also. Upon pikes of iron the heads of those who disregarded his ways were placed so on each corner and every street of the Blood Works reminders of his works lay. The few who made it to fifteen years would then be granted the honour of leaving the relative safety of the Blood Works to venture out to the parts of this isle their kind had little power over. The Tainted Land is what they named it, fog covered and dead the land was, while the air choked any who inhaled it. Few dare take on this feat for the Keeper of the Ways created it to be an impossibility and none who took on this trial had ever returned triumphant. A fact he knew well when their chief Valcea Ash fell gravely ill and while he lay under his blankets slowly fading with his two young sons beside him the Keeper of the Ways, along with others plotted. Drawn by howling the pair of brothers left their father's bedside to be met by the Keeper of the Ways. 'He's had it now, your father is done, the line of Ash done with it. So the ways say by the word of the Dark Lord the line of Ash is forever finished,' he snarled to the pair. About him those of the Horitin blood line and their grunts gathered and soon surrounded the two brothers. Others still loyal to their ailing chief stepped forward to aid them. Sadly their voices were not enough to quell the Keeper of the Ways, but were enough to force a compromise. 'Let the ways of the Master speak for the dead. Let them face the Tainted Lands. Eighty days did our Master toil to birth our forbears, so eighty days must the oldest Ash last. If he returns we will honour their line, but if he fails like all others have, the line of Horitin shall rule. Scarred by the Master they have been, but his hand of wrath their ancestor's once were. To glory they will lead our horde.' With the challenge set the oldest Ash brother was taken and lead away while his brother screamed obscenities at those who forced them apart.

With bound hands and covered eyes his shoes were removed and he was forced to walk over the sharp volcanic rocks that covered the plains of the Blood Works. Until the eldest brother saw a white mist covering his bloody feet from under the blindfold. Suddenly his hands were freed and he was pushed to the floor. 'Run now runt, run fast and run far on your stumps,' Oshan Horitin bellowed as his foot pushed the eldest brother's head into the dirt beneath the mist. When he rose from the mud he was alone and all about him the mist wafted. Thankfully Valcea Ash had not coddled his young so into the mist the boy went leaving footprints of dark green blood as he strode on. The air slowed him but only slightly. Soon after entering the mist his throat became numb from inhaling the toxic air.

The sounds of the beasts the mist concealed echoed around him, but on he went as the howls and gnashing teeth made his eyes dart back and forth. Breaking a branch from a fallen tree he fastened it into a spear just as the mist parted and the gnashing sound grew louder. The drool falling from the monster's mouth is what he saw first, his eyes followed the huge line of running saliva to a mouth, containing teeth sharp enough to cleave through dwarves true gold. A monster of myth this was for no other had seen the red eyes and spiked back it wielded and lived. Grey was its leathery skin letting it fade back into the mist, but in the mist it's red eyes glowed like lanterns. Letting the eldest watch and ready his arm as it encircled him, not thinking to watch his back. Never do the mist monsters prowl alone and while distracted by one the other moved to his back and pounced.

However the monsters soon realised not only they had been hunting the eldest brother. Another had been following footprints of blood so when the mist monster sprang it was met with a cold blade hewing the head of the beast. 'Away with you monsters for the Ash brothers are no prey for demons,' Ore Ash the youngest brother declared upon the corpse of the slain monster. Away the glowing eyes went and a sword was thrust into the eldest's hand. 'This is not your burden to bear,' Mor Ash stated readying to scold his younger brother. 'Brothers we are Mor and together do we face our burdens. Besides I must ensure you return for who else will throttle the Keeper and his foul ways,' Ore said as the sound of gnashing teeth returned along with many more sets of shining red eyes. Every trial they faced had prepared them for this, continuous beatings had made their skin tough. Endless days of training with steel made each swing of their blades deadly. Months of back breaking labour left them able to endure any torture, while their throats had been forced to swallow far worse than the toxic air. In waves the monster of the mist attacked, springing from the fog in increasing numbers time and time again. For days they harassed the brothers and for days they kept them at bay until all of a sudden the red eyes that stalked them vanished.

'Hurry and see to your cuts, we don't know how long we have until they return,' Mor ordered.

'Thirty seven days I'd say, that's how long they have been trying to put us on their dinner table. Why would they give up now?' Ore wondered aloud. Beneath the mist covering the floor both then noticed pebbles jumping over the ground. The sound of thumping footsteps followed and passed the bodies of slain mist monsters, within the swirling mist a colossal black shadow approached. Deathstomp the Trampler over twenty feet tall this cyclops was, with flesh as tough as steel. His great eye saw the brothers and the defeated mist monsters about them. 'Who dares walk my lands?' His booming voice bellowed from the mist. 'Shall I tell him brother, or do you wish the glory of plucking out his eye?'

'I have no name to give this one,' Mor roared back. 'No lands of giants are these, begone from the mist monster, this isle has only one master and he is of the Ash.'

'Orc are but ants to me boy. Nothing but bugs infesting my home,' Deathstomp yelled rising the tremendous club he wielded. 'The last of many am I, but I shall not flee the bugs as they.' The mist parted and the club fell separating the brothers and throwing both aside. Gripped by a massive hand

86

Ore then was, but his brother's sword thrown to Deathstomp's wrist forced him to drop his prey before he was able to crush his bones. Breaking a tooth from a dead mist monster Mor leapt to the great arm. One stab from the tooth made Deathstomp drop his colossal weapon, the next caused him to wail as Ore joined his older brother and pinned the cyclops's left foot to the ground with his sword. Deathstomp's arms flayed but was unable to stop the bug scurrying up his arm and planting an almighty punch right on the end of his nose. With one foot pinned he soon began to stumble making the mighty cyclops fall back. The ground broke apart beneath his huge frame as he stuck the earth but even with the floor breaking beneath them the brothers managed to regroup. 'Hurry we should finish him,' Mor stated.

'No,' Ore said running ahead of his brother to Deathstomp's great eye. 'What do you mean no? It will eat us,' Mor said.

'Remember father's word's brother. A defeated foe can be a great friend Mor,' Ore replied as Deathstomp stared to the pair.

Eighty days and eighty nights passed and those of the Blood Works waited before the Tainted Lands. None there expected Mor Ash to return. When he did the Keeper of the Ways raged after he saw not one, but two emerge from the mist. The skin of the mist monsters they wore, each wielding blunt and broken blades coated in the dried blood of the many they'd slew to survive. 'Cheated,' the Keeper of the Ways yelled. 'Only the eldest was meant to go.'

'But both survived, so both must be worthy,' a voice in the crowd added.

'No, no Ash shall rule. Valcea Ash is dead as will be his kin,' the Master declared but then a figure in the mist silenced the Keeper and all others. The ground shook and in the mist a great shadow watched the brothers returning home. 'True my brother did not face the Tainted Lands alone. For that was never the Keeper's task. To walk the plains of mist for eighty days and their nights was his trial. Never did he say my brother must do this alone,' Ore stated before the horde with the great figure to his back. 'Cheated and hung from the gallows they should be, the ways demand it,' the Keeper spat but those of the Horitin line had now left his side. 'Your ways are old Keeper, old enough to die I'd say. Let the horde have its new Master and let your ways and your shadows pass to the mist,' Ore said. Taking the Keeper by the ear he marched him before the swirling mist. 'Go now Keeper. For my brother's first act is that you must face all the many trials your ways have made you set over the years. Starting with this one,' Ore's boot sent the Keeper of the Ways tumbling into the mist where flickering red eyes would soon find him.

With the Keeper gone the line of Horitin fled and Mor Ash first son of Valcea Ash was set to take his father's place and begin his reign, but to the shock of many the eldest didn't take the mantle that waited for him. Instead he passed it, for in his kin he saw a chief mightier than even the dreaded Valcea Ash. A leader that would lead the horde to the greatest glory those of the Blood Works have ever known. This decision though didn't dampen the celebration that followed and they honoured him as you'd imagine orcs would. With beer, pork and many awful songs they praised him, but both brothers had been taken from the festivities. To the underground they were taken by the oldest of their kin. Withered was her skin and she spoke as if she was close to death. Elder Utter most called her and she lead the brothers down tunnels and through chasms that lay beneath the ground until they reached a hall containing many pits. In the largest of these holes the brothers were sent to retrieve a book buried at the bottom. Within the truth of the orcs and shadows was written. 'It is all your father and his could discover,' Elder Utter told the pair. 'Not born like elves from stars are we, nor born of this world. Made we were, made to serve a master who only ever wished us to be weapons for his shadows. In these pits the first were made, from a mixture of blood and bones stolen from others, that is what created our kin. Read its words and learn them well, the both of you. For one day the Dark Seer will return and death is all our race will know once more if you two cannot keep him from power. Hear this though and hear it well. A shadow will he send for the Dark Seer is just a mask that hides our true creator.'

Remade the Blood Works then was and the
Keeper's ways were soon forgotten alike Elder
Utter's warnings. A peaceful and tranquil time the
start of Ore Ash's reign was remembered as and
over the years that followed the Blood Works
flourished, but return the shadows did. Marched
through the dirt streets of the Blood Works to Ore
a shadow was by one of the banished Horitin no
less. Ore was forced to bow and the shadows ruled
his kind once more. Away hunting Mor had been
when the shadow arrived and upon his return
found those of the Blood Works marching to war.
'Where do you march to?' He yelled to a grunt
who ran by. 'Orashon, the Master wishes it
reclaimed, says its ripe for the taking,' the grunt
replied. 'Where is Ore? This is madness,' Mor
said. 'He's already gone ahead with the first wave,'
the orc replied before he was pushed aside and
Mor rushed down the line of soldiers to find his
brother. Boats had already carried hundreds over
the sea to the Screaming Skulls. There a sixty mile
march lay ahead, over terrain that made the Blood
Works seem idyllic. Passed it the tall walls of
Orashon lay and for years the dwarves of this city
had driven back any who approached from the

west. Row after row of cannons and mechanical defences covered the walls and even the sight of a single orc would make all fire. When Mor finally reached the field before Orashon only death did he find. Cannon fire had killed hundreds, torn corpses scattered the ground while blood dripped from dead splinted trees. Seeing his brother Mor ran to him and yelled. 'Send them home, stop this slaughter its needless you don't want Orashon.'

'But we do brother, we must,' Ore replied. 'It is the shadow's will and we are cursed to obey.' Thrown back Mor then was by an orc in a wolf shaped helm that concealed his deformed face. 'Oshan, you whelk. I'll rip your traitorous head off,' Mor spat.

'You're the only one speaking treason here Mor. The shadows have returned and in blood we will bathe them,' Oshan declared and rose the axe he wielded. With that the next wave of warriors ran forth and the cannons fired once again. 'Stop this, it's pointless there's no glory here,' Mor insisted. None paid him any heed and he soon realised there was no stopping this, but he wondered. *Maybe I could end it.* Pushing passed the others he ran to join the charging warriors. Cannon balls fell scarring those about him and alone he soon went. Scooping a rock from the ground Mor leapt to the wall and as the sounds of firing cannons faded he climbed the jagged bricks. Daring to look back Mor saw how high he'd climbed along with another wave of warriors readying to run through the mangled corpses of the last. Reaching the first row of cannons he used the rock he'd carried under his belt to block the barrel and then continued to climb. Oshan's axe was raised again and orcs ran this time however cannon balls didn't rain down. Only a couple reached the charging warriors the rest bore witness to a sight they would sing songs about. The cannons had fired but the blocked barrel made it explode from within, setting alight the black powder stored inside the wall. Sending a cascade of detonations over the defences turning the many cannons to scrap metal and allowing others to reach the wall and witness Mor upon the battlements. Fire torn up about him from the burning war machines as he battled the defenders of Orashon alone. Mor the Mighty all who saw him named him and to his back ladders fell and the Blood Works rallied. With their vast defences destroyed most fled the city to the east. While

93

those who stayed died fighting or were taken prisoner and forced into the service of the Master Ore Ash now served.

The streets of the dwarven city filled and a gallows was built upon which Oshan named himself executioner and went about his new calling with glee. A man with black cloth covering his face and body watched on with Ore Ash to his side. To the back of the crowd Mor stood none too impressed with Oshan's bloody show. Until one dwarf was brought forward and forced to his knees, this dwarf was the only one who the Dark Seer's shadow showed an interest in. Watching him rise from his seat Mor strained his ears to try and hear what the dwarf was saying, but all he could make out was a stutter. 'W, w, wat,' is all Mor could hear before his head fell from his shoulders and Oshan declared to the crowd. 'This city is ours and now to the elves we will look. To the Cove we ride and there those of Meceller will be taken and pulled upon the gallows like the rest.' When the crowd turned to march on they found their way blocked. 'We have our prize let it be, we need no more blood,' Mor's pleas only lead to chains being wrapped around his wrists as those loyal to Oshan set on him. Bound and beaten Mor was and as the Blood Work's horde marched he was forced to see the horrific sights that unfolded at the Cove as they went. Until one day he woke after being knocked unconscious to find himself surrounded by tall oaks and slain wolves.

The

Dragon

and his

Phoenix

Stolen Tales

Fire mages unlike others are remarkably rare or so the centaur Professor Carny believed, that was until he found two. Since opening the Ranger's Academy the Headmistress there had been instructing all of her teachers to bring any who possess magical abilities to the safety of the academy. In a vain attempt to save the young souls from the Countess of Accultian's callous hands. The first Professor Carny found was a young girl, Flora Teffal was her name. A wood elf girl with long, light brown hair and a pair of round glasses resting on her nose above her freckled cheeks she is. Who the humble Professor found purely by chance. While trotting to Hannerson on one of his regular strolls he smelt burning, then saw black smoke bellowing into the sky from a barn that was ablaze. Running to it he found a pair wailing before the burning building. Their only child had ran into the fire to free the horses kept there. Sure she was lost they mourned like you'd imagine, but as the flames filled the doorway their daughter simply walked through. Not burnt or even singed was her body. Totally unharmed by the flames, she ran to her parents who found a well dressed centaur to their back asking about the girl's education. The second he found after a tip from the Headmistress, Consor Rackie. A stray he was or that is what those of Duniesa would call the homeless such as he. For not all of the Seer's city is fair and in the slums Consor was making a worrying name for a boy of only fourteen. Ignoring these rumours Professor Carny offered him a place at the Academy an offer young Consor eagerly accepted.

Not long did it take for the pair to bond, making their years at the academy pass in blissful seconds. Only a handful of years after leaving the Academy did they have their son, a fine happy child he was, but neither Professor Carny or our mages knew anything about what lay ahead. For another's eyes had watched the pair for years, through the Seeker's Stones. Two ancient black orbs that he replaced his eyes with. Allowing him to watch the world from the prison he'd been trapped within. In all his years of watching he found none to his taste, but now seeing Flora he grew fond of her and with her beauty reaching its prime he would take her for his own. Into her room shadows crept and before

Consor's return she was taken. Leaving her child wailing in his crib as she was pulled through closed windows and carried away into the night.

'Who could do this Professor, who?' Consor raged after returning to the Ranger's Academy with his son. 'There is only one who could, Tillamun is his name and no mage more vile will you find,' the Professor said. 'You need not go. I love her also, as a daughter, but you need not go. Think to Ernest, think to what she'd want for her son.'

'Ernest shall be safe with you Professor, as we were. I shall not leave her to whatever fate this Tillamun has imagined,' Consor replied.

'A blade you will need then,' the Professor said gesturing to a closet. Opening it he retrieved two short swords of dwarves true gold these were, with silver pommels on the ends. Each held a different symbol in the centre. 'You were both so young when I had these made, here this one is yours,' he said handing Consor the sword with the dragon emblem. 'Not really a woods elf's friend, a dragon I mean,' Consor said.

The Dragon and his Phoenix

'It will remind you to not let your fury overcome you, don't let the emotions the flames bring create the man you are and give this to Flora for me. The phoenix is for her and I beg you come back to me as bright as they would.'

To the sea Consor went, sailing to the shattered isles where Tillamun's Tower was said to lay. Months had already passed but now finally his boat found shore and he walked to stand before the tower. Black it was with many spires about it and grim creatures hovering above. With nothing to conceal himself Consor was soon set on by these winged beasts. Balls of fire knocked them from the sky as they swarmed him. A master of his art Consor had become and so around his arms bright flames cut down his enemies until none were left. All was quiet until Tillamun spoke and Consor could hear only his ghastly voice echoing. 'Who dares disturb the Master of the Damned, the ruler of the world between life and death.' The foul voice rang out stinging Consor's ears. 'I do, for you have stolen from me mage and I will take back my love,' Consor yelled.

'Your love, oh but you mean my betrothed, my Flora. For her beauty and her body are now mine, no mere mortal can challenge me here. Begone.'

'I shall not begone, show yourself coward. Open the doors to your keep and stand before me if you are so mighty,' Consor replied making the echoing voice laugh. 'So be it.' With that the earth cracked and began to break apart making the black tower sink into the ground pulling Consor into the darkness with it.

Waking all about Consor was black, summoning a flame to his hand didn't help. Trapped in a chasm of pitch black was he. The ground he noticed was purple and sticky to touch with no clear path. Luckily a guide was to hand, one who had waited years for one of the living to dare go against Tillamun. 'Finally one who is still bone and flesh.' A voice from Consor's back made him spin. There he found a short fat man using a broken staff as a cane. A huge messy beard covered his face but that didn't hide the grin beneath it. 'Finally, oh yes and about time I'd say.'

'Who are you?' Consor asked.

'A friend dear lad, but a guide, yes. That's what you'll probably see me as. Where you are though that is what should worry a living lad like yourself,' the short man replied.

'I have not the time for this I must find Flora where is she?' Consor said.

'Ah love,' the man chuckled. 'What else would drive one to seek this madness, come along then,' the man said beginning to walk off. Seeing no other alternative Consor followed and then asked. 'Where are you leading me fool?'

'Fool tuh, I am leading you to this Flora taken by Tillamun she is yes?' He snapped.

'Yes,' Consor replied.

'So on the highest level she will be. I can guide you but none have travelled all the levels and left this place.'

'How could you have survived so long here and know so much if it's so impossible?' Consor argued. 'Because like all others here I am not of the living,' the man said halting and tapping his cane to the ground. Glowing lights then began approaching them from ahead, drawing closer quickening as it went. Cries of anguish followed until they were screaming in Consor's ears. 'What is it?' He asked.

'The moat of the damned. Here Tillamun casts the souls of the damned and full the moat has gotten over the years.' Back to the light Consor's eyes went to see it came from a boat. Made from blackened wood, with the figure of a hellish beast at the head. The boat though mattered little when Consor saw what it sailed through. Hundreds wailed as it plowed through a mass of stolen souls. Pale their bodies were, with faces that only possessed a mouth to ensure they endlessly continue to drown on the vile the moat contained. 'Who would dream of such a thing, let alone make it,' Consor said retching from the sight. 'This is but the start, too late you are to turn back now so on you must go,' the short man said as he boarded the boat. 'Who are you?' Consor asked. 'What was it? Before my face and name were taken by another. What did they call me? Ah yes, June that was it, yes the weary Wizard June that is what most called me.'

'You, you created the humans with Elidom, you're the one who cast them away,' Consor said.

'No,' June snapped. 'That was another, but forget her and her lies let us go.' The boat then pulled away, it didn't have a crew or any oars but sailed on all the same. 'So you are dead?' Consor asked. 'Yes, like all others who are here. Tillamun uses the Seeker's Stones to trap souls travelling to the Nexus,' June said.

'A Nexus, Seeker's Stones I have so many questions,' Consor said.

'Ones I will answer, but our first trial draws close and I can only help here with advice. Such as with this opponent you're best striking first.' With that June's body faded leaving Consor to discover what pulled the boat.

Ahead was a great ladder the size of which a titan could climb. Before it a colossal horned beast pulled on a chain that dragged the boat through the damned souls. 'Who's this?' The monster cried out. 'I am Consor Rackie let me by,' Consor yelled to the beast as his hands trembled. 'Pass, no, my Master will not allow it,' the beast roared reaching into the moat of souls and revealing a mace he had concealed beneath. Thanks to June's warning

Consor knew he had to act fast. Running to the end of the boat Consor drew the swords Professor Carny had gifted him. As the colossal began to rise Consor leapt from the figure head of the boat. Orange flames ran down his arms and consumed the swords as he slammed them into the rising head. 'Die monster, for none shall stand in my way. None shall keep me from Flora,' Consor declared as fire shot from the swords making the horned monsters melting brains pour from its putrid ears. Upon the dead beast Consor stood as the damned drowned around him. Then he wondered if this monster pulled the boat here who was it that pulled it back. His eyes rose and his heart quickened even more as waves began to rock the boat and the roar of the second colossal rang out over the rippling moat. With a few great bounds he was before the boat, smashing through it the beast swung its axe. Powerful was this blow but slow and obvious were his movements allowing Consor to dodge the swing of the giant axe. Letting it embed itself in the corpse of the other. Leaping onto the axe Consor ran to the monster's hand and with a spin of flames and steel the beast's fingers were cut. Dropping his axe the colossal stumbled back his arm alight with flames controlled by Consor. The fires burnt their way up his arm burrowing into his chest, turning the towering colossal's insides to ash until its body crumbled into pieces.

'It seems wood folk are more powerful than in my day,' June said reappearing.

'You. Where did you go?' Consor said.

'I told you I can only be your guide. Tillamun's monsters are flesh and blood like yourself, but me. I am no different than the souls in the moat,' June said.

'Then why do you not join them? What makes you so special?' Consor asked.

'I was not sent here by Tillamun's command and have hidden from his sight, until now. You cannot fail lad for if you do he will surely put me in worse places than the moat. On now save your strength for the climb.'

Up the impending ladder Consor went climbing up for hours until finally he saw a ridge and grew even more irritated with his guide when he realised June had simply reappeared at the top. Pulling himself up the smell hit him before the foul sight. Pink creatures, two foot high with sharp teeth and long chipped nails ran around piles of bones and mangled flesh. 'What hell scape have you lead me to now?' Consor asked.

'The second level, the assembly room. See there, the runts collect the bones to make Tillamun's flayed ones,' June said.

'Flayed ones?' Consor asked.

'Fallen warriors who Tillamun gifts bodies of bones to, you shall meet them soon enough,' June said. 'What more lays before us? Tell me,' Consor demanded. 'Do you not wish to find your love, your Flora? If I tell you of the countless horrors that inhabit this place will you flee, is that it?' June snapped.

'No, I will carry on through any madness to find her,' Consor said.

'Then trust in your guide,' June stated. Going on the runts seemed none too interested in them, more concerned with their work they were. 'It's strange we must have been here a day or more now but I'm yet to feel hungry or even tired,'

Consor said. 'It is Tillamun's doing, within the space between life and death he created a new realm. Here he makes his torrid dreams reality,' June told him. 'I can't imagine any dreaming up anything like this,' Consor said.

'In the image of a god they say high elves like he were made, makes me wonder what sordid desires Norcea truly had, never mind that. Look there, up ahead lays your path,' June said. He had lead Consor to the grinding pits. There great mincers and forks sorted bone from flesh. Its operator though was Consor's concern. Behind a mess of pulleys and levers a bloated torso had been welded to a metal frame. 'Wizard, what wizard?' The head sewn ontop yelled through a tube connected to a series of bronze dishes. 'Any advice?' Consor asked but June had already vanished. Levers were pulled and forks moved from the pits stabbing for Consor. Leaving him dodging strikes while trying to avoid being knocked into one of the many gruesome pits. Suddenly a mechanical hand clasped him and held him aloft over one. 'So this is the pest troubling the Master, how did you get passed the boat pullers?' The voice of the operator reverberated from the dishes. 'I killed those monsters as I will you, if you do not release me and let me pass,' Consor replied. 'Mm, the Master won't like that he won't, it's the mincer for you,' the operator said yanking on a pulley to release the hand's grip. Consor though was nimble grabbing hold of the hand, as he fell he drew his sword and leapt back to the platform as more forks were directed towards him. 'Jumpy little cockroach ain't ya,' the operator yelled as Consor swiped at his mechanisms. None the operator believed could break his mechanical contraptions but Consor's blade now cleaved through them with ease. 'Enough of this.' With a great roaring bellow the operator pulled on the largest lever before him, making steam pour out from pipes all about the grinding pits. As the steam cleared from the pipes the pink creatures poured through in incredible numbers. Running to the operator Consor soon had his sword to the vile thing's throat. 'Send them back,' he demanded. In a sickening laugh the operator responded. 'There's no sending them back, they'll eat ya alive.' With a flick of Consor's sword the operator was beheaded but his sick laugh continued as his head rolled into a pit.

Running from the torrent of chatters chasing him Consor went until he reached a ledge. 'Go, jump,' June said reappearing.

'Are you crazy? I cannot even see the bottom.'

'It is the door to the next level you must jump,' June ordered again and with the creatures approaching Consor saw little choice. Leaping from the edge he was quickly engulfed by the darkness leaving the creatures chattering on the ledge behind.

Consor didn't plummet to the ground as he expected, instead after his initial fall he began to float down slowly. Finally after hours of floating he landed on a thin cobble path. 'Quickly lad light your way as best you can,' June said but on this level his form had faded. 'Where are you wizard?' Consor yelled as he held aloft his flaming sword to light his way. Even with his torch the darkness remained all around him, the fire was only able to light the narrow path. 'Go quick. Here is where Tillamun keeps the souls of the murdered. The darkness stops myself and them from taking our true form. Little can I help now, but to tell you once you begin walking you cannot stop or look away, lest you lose your way in the darkness.' June's voice then faded leaving Consor alone to walk the path. Only a few steps did he take before the path grew thinner until just one stone lay before the next. The cries then started as the murdered spirits around him began to make themselves known. 'Murderer,' the damned cried about him. Grey smoke started to follow Consor forming shapes to try and draw his eyes from the path. Their attempts thankfully failed until a voice Consor knew cried out. 'Murderer, damned murderer Consor Rackie.'

'I know that voice,' Consor mumbled but didn't take his eyes from the path. 'Lewis is that you?'

'You know it's me brother, or do you forget all those you burn in the infernos you create?' Lewis said, while the grey smoke formed a house that followed Consor as he walked. 'You forget me, you forget them.'

'I never did, I swear I never,' Consor replied. 'Liar. you forgot the moment we burnt and now you cannot even look upon your heinous deeds,' Lewis said.

'Stop this brother, you know I cannot look,' Consor said as the grey flames set the house ablaze. Leaving the sounds of the ones inside burning to death to ring in Consor's ears. 'Look upon it brother, see your truth. For no saviour or loving father are you. But a killer is all you are, a murderer damned to relive their deaths forever more,' Lewis's voice crackled as the grey flames surrounded Consor until all his victims followed him down the fading path. 'I did not know, how was I to,' Consor mumbled as the scarred face of his mother flashed before his eyes. His father followed, then his sister and finally his brother, whose burning face roared at him as it flashed by. The shock knocked Consor to his knees and as his pace slowed the path before him vanished. Cupping his head in his hands he rocked back and forth in the darkness as his murdered family tormented him. Another murdered soul though now wandered the darkness and had been searching for Consor ever since finding himself lost in this void. The voices plaguing Consor fled as another echoed out of the dark. 'Begone you fiends, for a child cannot be blamed for your deaths. Begone before I see his fires banish what's left of you.' The voice sent waves of relief over Consor as his head rose, and before him the ghostly figure of Professor Carny stood. 'P... Professor. How are you here? No, Ernest is he safe? What has happened?' Consor asked.

'Murdered I was, but safe your son is, safe and from what I have seen thriving. Much time has passed since you left my friend. Worry for that once you and our beloved Flora leave this place. I know the path you seek, follow close and keep your eyes on me,' Professor Carny said.

'What has happened since I left?' Consor asked.

'The world has gone to war Consor, a war myself and others long suspected would come,' Professor Carny told him. 'And he is, Ernest is safe, yes?' Consor asked.

'The last I saw of him he was, but worry for yourself my old student. Here the next door lies and I must leave you now,' the Professor said as a light rose before them until with a burst of light a golden door stood in front of the pair. 'Wait if you leave I will not see you again,' Consor said.

'It is sadly so, but do not leave me with sadness my mage. Go with a happy heart one you will share with our Flora. Passed this door Tillamun's Tower lies. He will have summoned all he can to guard him there. Expect a battle unlike any you have fought before,' Professor Carny said as the grey smoke faded and left Consor alone before the doorway.

Shoving open the golden doors Consor found the Wizard June waiting on the other side. 'What took you so long? You looked away didn't you?' He said. 'I am here am I not, wherever here even is,' Consor replied. 'Wizard,' a voice bellowed out from on top of the tower before the pair. A large rickety bridge lay before it and below a river of flowing lava ran. Either side of the bridge two colossals upon large boulders stood. An army of flayed ones covered the bridge and in the sky winged monsters flew screeching as they went. 'How dare you lead him here Wizard, but now I see you clearly and you will be damned like the rest,' Tillamun bellowed from the plateau on top of his tower. 'Damned you will be and a whole new realm of discomfort will I create for you. As for he, his soul will be forced to watch his love with another for all of time.'

'I shall take your head Tillamun and my love. For I have beaten all you have and I will cut through all these too,' Consor yelled back as he drew his swords and flames engulfed his arms. With a wave of Tillamun's hand the flayed ones charged and the monsters in the sky descended. 'I shall buy you mere seconds, be ready.' Rising up before Consor, June yelled. 'Go now Consor, win your love.' The light growing in June's chest then exploded blinding the charging monsters and from this great light a dragon of flames burst through. Tearing at the deformed titan on the left of the bridge, as Consor ran to the flayed ones. Phoenix ablaze with a red flame, his free hand sent forth Consor's rage. Screaming skulls of flames consumed the monsters as flayed knights were released from their torture by his blade. Beheaded and alight the titan fell striking the bridge as he went. With a click of Consor's fingers the flaming dragon faded and his sword was released from the dragon form he'd created. It flew back to his hand while the bridge began to crumble behind him. Leaping to the door as the last piece of the bridge fell, he used his swords to stab through the iron door and hold himself there as the second titan swung his mace. Slow like the others he was letting Consor pull his feet up onto the handle of his sword and then jumped into the air as the mace slammed into the door shaking the tower. 'He's in the tower stop him,' Tillamun yelled as flayed ones clanged about the spire in their bent steel. Unaware Consor hadn't entered the door, instead he climbed the colossal's huge arm setting the beast ablaze as he went. With the beast dead he rode upon the falling corpse so he was thrown onto the plateau beside Tillamun. 'Where is she? Where is Flora?' Consor yelled. 'You have no weapon fire mage you can't beat me with your fire al..,' Tillamun was cut off by the phoenix slicing through his left arm. The dragon then followed removing his right and both returned to Consor's hands. 'Where is she?' Consor said with a voice full of rage, holding his sword to Tillamun's neck, but only a callous laugh came from his enemy. As Tillamun's head rose Consor realised he only had one eye. 'She's gone, dead. You wasted your life here mage, all your trials and she's already dead. Not so meek was she for as soon as I returned with her she fought me and destroyed my eye. Then to the woods she went,' Tillamun said. 'What woods? Where are these woods? Tell me,' Consor demanded.

'A wood I made of all those who take their own life. A tree of flesh she will become. Go, the door sits at the foot of my throne room. Go die with her,' Tillamun laughed still.

'I shall find her and end all of your madness.' With that Consor thrust the dragon through Tillamun's remaining eye, ending him and destroying the last Seeker's Stone.

Before the corpse of his foe Consor stood as joy filled cries echoed around him and June appeared to his side. 'You hear it, hear them. The damned are being freed and sent on all over.'

'What of you, why do you remain?' Consor asked. 'Because you are still here to guide, we shall find your love yet lad,' June said.

'What if he spoke the truth and she truly is gone?' Consor said.

The Dragon and his Phoenix

'What if, what if. What if you do find her and then are both eaten by some monster? What if you find her and she no longer wants you? What if your life has been a wasted endeavour? Will you let what ifs slow you now?' June said. Realising he would go on no matter what, Consor descended the now empty tower. Passed the bones of the flayed ones until he came to a door overgrown with foliage.

Burning it down Consor passed through to a wood that was once filled with the souls of those who took their own life. In cases of unbreakable wood they were kept but now only one tree remained. 'No, my dear Flora, it can't be.' There she stood encased in bark. 'She can't have. She just can't have done this to herself. It's not true,' Consor raged as he tried to burn the bark away. 'Time's passing so differently on each level, who knows how long she waited for you here,' June said placing his ghostly hand to the bark. 'Why does she remain? Why does she still have to suffer?' Consor said as tears flowed from his eyes. A smile then found June and he said. 'She's not dead, just consumed by what was about her she was.' He then turned to Consor with the same smile. 'I'm done now, my guiding is done lad for the time being anyhow. Good luck to you Consor, for I fear more than these horrors wait for you and your love passed here, but free from here you will be. So I say good luck and goodbye.' With that June tapped his cane to the floor. A great white light engulfed him and he was gone. Replaced by a vision of what was now the past. Within the vision Consor saw a boy upon the marble walls of the Seer's city Duniesa. Surrounded by purple clad soldiers and seemed destined to die, Consor then realised this was their son, it was Ernest. 'No June. Why show us such a thing I don't wish to see my son's death,' Consor cried looking away. Thankfully his love didn't and even from within her shell she saw her son falling, but he didn't stay down long. For a female warrior bounded towards him. An orc she was with flowing black hair and as she fought Flora's son looked to her. Rising, his hands became engulfed in flames, but not any her or Consor had seen before. White these flames were, white flames that fed on the undying love that bonded the pair. Showing Flora their strength not

The Dragon and his Phoenix only came from the rage that wielding the flames creates. More images then filled Flora's mind ones of Consor's trials and his journey to find her. The sights filled her heart and lit a white light within it. White flames spawned and her heart pumped them around her body. Before her Consor wept until the smell of burning bark found him and he looked up to see Flora freeing herself from the cage that trapped her. 'You took your time my dragon,' she said as her mouth was revealed. Jumping up from the ground his hands found her face and his lips hers. 'My love, my Phoenix. I started to believe I'd never hold you again,' Consor said. While the bark burnt in the white flames the pair embraced until finally free Flora said. 'Reunited we are, but not complete are we yet.'

'You're right let us leave here, find our son and be a family once more,' Consor said.

'I know the way your guide showed me,' Flora told him.

Hand in hand they went through the barren plain that the woods had become, until they found a black door in the centre. 'Are you sure this is the exit?' Consor asked.

'It is what your guide showed me, I don't know what's passed it,' Flora said. She then felt Consor take hold of her hips as he attached the phoenix to her belt. 'Whatever is there we shall face it and find our son together,' Consor told her. Holding tight to one another they opened the door and the last souls to dwell in Tillamun's cursed hell scape were freed.

Neither had any idea what to expect and when the light faded, both found themselves bemused at what they saw. Before them a human in a black uniform sat upon a wolf with a mechanical leg. Slamming the book he read from closed the human said to them. 'About time you two got here.'

'Where are we?' Consor asked as more warriors appeared around them. All of different creeds they were, some even looked to be from other worlds. 'The end of the world dragon mage,' the human replied. 'Follow the wolf and together we may just survive.'

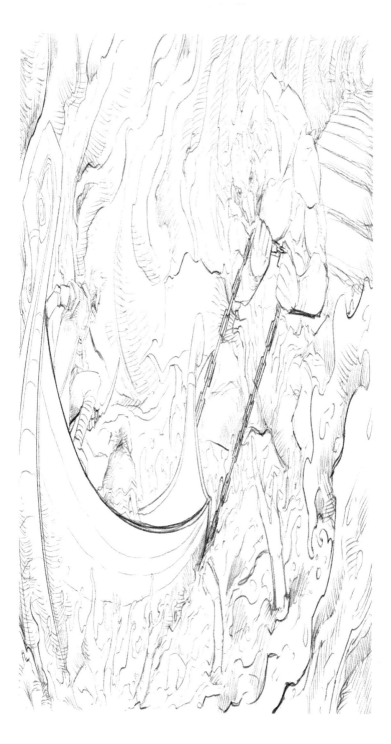

'I don't want company,' Seer Avlor Tranem snapped as another sat across from him. 'Why so rude Seer? I just wish to play a game,' Wasiz the Rotting Thief replied pulling back his black hood and taking the smoking pipe from his mouth. 'To intrude on one's dinner is far more ill mannered than my reply. Be off and let me eat, I don't wish to play any of your games,' Avlor said.

'So sure, but you don't even know what game I wish to play,' Wasiz chuckled revealing a golden coin in his hand. Turning it to reveal the head of King Elidom Godborn on one side and the griffin Charlemagne on the other he said. 'Heads I win a favour from you, tails you get the prize I've hidden. A prize that would fit nicely in that vault of yours.'

'What could you have for the vault?' Avlor asked. 'Tut tut Avlor,' Wasiz said waggling his finger. 'That's not the game, nor can you ask what the favour is I wish for, even without your gift of foresight I see what your next question will be.'

'Fine then,' Avlor said dropping his knife and fork. 'Let us play your game. I feel you will not leave me in peace until I do.' With that Wasiz flicked the coin high and let it drop back down onto the back of his hand. 'It's heads I win,' Wasiz chuckled showing off the coin as Avlor cursed his luck and began to worry what the thief may ask of him. 'It's a heist isn't it, some sort of silliness you wish to drag me into,' Avlor said.

'Nothing so exciting I'm afraid my Seer, a simple favour is all I seek,' Wasiz replied.

'So what will it be,' Avlor asked.

'Years will pass, me and my friends will be forgotten, or worse. I don't know how it will happen if the Headmistress or Balmoth will bring them, but one day a choice will be put to you and your Seers. A decision regarding the fate of two brothers. When this happens you must ensure they continue on. Lie if you must, but they must be admitted to the Ranger's Academy,' Wasiz stated.

'A grand thief you are chain breaker, but even you cannot steal the future,' Avlor said.

'I don't aim to steal it, just nudge it in the direction I wish it to go. Do I have your word Seer?' Wasiz asked.

'I doubt the time will ever come, but if it does I will do as you ask. Now do tell, what is it you have for the vaults?' Avlor asked.

'A book, one with a black cloth cover that holds no name, but sadly you lost my Seer. So with that I say good day and trust you'll keep your word,' Wasiz said while puffing on his pipe. Leaving the coin on the table he strolled to the door in a cloud of smoke letting Avlor return to his dinner. Reaching over the table Avlor picked up the coin and noticed as he did each side was the same as the other. 'That cheat,' Avlor chuckled to himself but before he could tuck back into the scrumptious leek and potato pie before him the possible name of the book Wasiz spoke of came to mind. 'The shadow scripts,' he yelped as he jumped up from his seat. Running to the door he went to rush after the Rotting Thief. Opening it though he saw the thief had already left the book behind. Sat on the porch floor it lay and Avlor's hands shook as he reached for it and hid it under his cape. To the high elf's vault it would be taken and there it was left to gather dust and be forgotten by all but one.

Continue your adventures in Alidor

Follow us on Instagram @alidorbooks

ALIDOR

THE FEAR THEY FEED ON

Printed in Great Britain
by Amazon

26731582R00076